Omelette: A chicken in peril!

Whatever you like to read,
Red Fox has got the story for you.
Why not choose another book from our range of
Animal Stories, Funny Stories or Fantastic Stories?
Reading has never been so much fun!

RED FOX ANIMAL STORIES

FOWL PEST

James Andrew Hall
illustrated by Lucy Case

RED FOX FUNNY STORIES

THANKS FOR THE SARDINE

Written and illustrated
by Laura Beaumont

GIZZMO LEWIS: FAIRLY SECRET AGENT

Michael Coleman

RED FOX FANTASTIC STORIES

THE STEALING OF QUEEN VICTORIA

Shirley Isherwood,
illustrated by George Buchanan

THE INFLATABLE SHOP

Willis Hall, illustrated by Babette Cole

Omelette: A chicken in peril!

Gareth Owen

RED FOX

For Natty from Fatty

A Red Fox Book

Published by Random House Children's Books
20 Vauxhall Bridge Road, London SW1V 2SA

A division of Random House UK Ltd
London Melbourne Sydney Auckland
Johannesburg and agencies throughout the world

1 3 5 7 9 10 8 6 4 2

First published in Great Britain by
The Bodley Head Children's Books 1990
Published in paperback by Red Fox 1991

This Red Fox edition 1999

Printed in Norway by AIT Trondheim AS

RANDOM HOUSE UK Limited Reg. No. 954009

ISBN 0 09 940013 8

One

Before he was even born Omelette had two pieces of pure luck. And that's more than most chickens get in a lifetime. The first was that when he fell tumbling out of the sky, that foggy November morning, he made a soft landing on a pile of yellow hay. The second piece of luck was that he landed on the Westmorelands' Farm. Mr and Mrs Westmoreland didn't believe in killing and eating animals. They drank the milk, they ate the eggs, they sheared the sheep, but they didn't believe in slaughtering animals for food. As Mr Westmoreland was fond of saying, 'My animals are my friends. How you could look a turkey or a hen or a sheep in the face and then see him roasted amongst potatoes, peas and sprouts of a Sunday lunch, I shall never know.'

So all the animals on the Westmorelands' farm lived safe, secure and happy.

On this particular morning Mrs Westmoreland was walking from the orchard with a heap of windfalls in her pinafore when she heard something landing in the hayrick. When she looked closer she saw a brown egg nestling there undamaged. She knew it hadn't been laid by one of her own hens.

'Where you come from?' she said.

She heard an angry chattering above her and, looking up, saw a magpie furious at losing his breakfast after flying with it in his beak for so many miles.

1

Mrs Westmoreland shook her fist at the magpie. 'You black and white thief,' she shouted. 'You stole this egg from somebody else's nest, didn't you?'

The magpie flew into a tall oak tree and sat there complaining bitterly to himself.

The farmer's wife slipped the egg, with the windfalls, into her pinafore and walked across the farmyard to the house, smiling. 'Make a nice omelette for my old man's breakfast,' she said to herself.

But when she cracked the shell over the bowl, instead of a golden yoke, a bedraggled bantam chick stuck his head out.

'Well I never!' exclaimed the farmer's wife. 'Fancy that now. A baby cockerel. Must be your lucky day, my love. If I hadn't had my wits about me, you'd have been inside my old man's stomach before you could say "omelette".'

And that, of course, is how Omelette came by his name.

His feathers were damp and scrawny and his eyes big with wonder. He stared round about him, then slid out of the rest of the egg. He tried to walk across the kitchen table but he had only tottered a step or two when he trod on a spoon, wrapped both legs round each other and fell flat on his face in a bowl of custard.

The farmer's wife dried him with a towel, then made a bed for him in an old cardboard box and kept him warm by the stove. Three times a day she fed him on warm milk from a teaspoon. Because she was the first moving thing Omelette had ever seen, Omelette decided that the farmer's wife must be his mother. That's how it is with chicks. As he grew older and stronger he would follow her around the kitchen, his little wings held out for balance. When he found his voice he learned to cheep whenever she spoke to him.

2

The farmer's wife would laugh. 'We're going to get you good and strong, then we'll put you out in the yard with the other creatures. We never had a bantam cock before.'

From outside in the yard came the hysterical clucking of hens, turkeys and geese followed by the thunder of hooves. The farmer looked out of the window and cursed. 'I'll be blowed, it's that there Eric after them hens again.'

He ran outside shouting and waving his stick.

Omelette bounded on to the windowsill and peered through the window. What a sight met his eyes! Four fat hens scuttled clucking about the yard chased by Eric the goat who in turn was chased by the farmer. Omelette bounced up and down, beat his wings and sang for joy. He had never seen such a proud, handsome creature in his life. How fine and brave it looked with its curved horns and its beard waving in the breeze. In that instant Omelette decided that's what he would be when he grew up. What could be finer or more exciting? For the next few months he dreamed of being a goat and chasing hens.

But his days in the warmth and comfort of the farmhouse kitchen were numbered. One day, Mr and Mrs Westmorelands' daughter, Jenny, visited the farm. She said to her mother, 'That there Omelette's getting spoiled in here. Reckon he's big enough and strong enough to face the world now.'

'Cheep, cheep,' said Omelette, who was sitting comfortably in Jenny's red beret. He understood a few words by now and wondered where this place called 'the World' could be.

The farmer's wife picked him up and placed him on the slate step outside the kitchen door. Omelette blinked in the cold sunlight and gazed about him. The door slammed and he was on his own in the outside world. A tractor roared by throwing dust and fumes into the air. Two large sheepdogs ran past yapping at a couple of stray sheep. Over by the pond the geese honked and flapped their wings.

Two large hens strutted over to inspect the new arrival. To Omelette, who was only a few months old, they seemed very large and imposing. They looked down their beaks at him. Omelette shivered. He had got used to the cosy ways of the kitchen where the farmer's wife did everything for him. He thought everybody was like her. He looked at the fattest hen.

'Good morning,' he said gravely. 'I'm rather cold, could you bring me some milk?'

'Hark at Lord Muck,' said the fat hen to her friend.

They walked round Omelette inspecting him closely.

'Look what the wind brought in,' said the other. 'What are you called when you're at home?'

'Omelette,' said Omelette.

'Omelette!' said the fat hen, sniggering. 'And where did you come from . . . Omelette?'

Omelette pointed straight up at the sky.

The hens stared up.

'From the sky?'

'Yes,' said Omelette.

'Was your mother an aeroplane then?' asked a turkey, joining in the fun.

This was too much for the hens. They roared. Soon there was quite a crowd round Omelette. The turkey became so helpless with laughter that two ducks had to hold her upright.

Omelette looked round seriously, 'No, I don't think my mother's an aeroplane.'

'Well, who brought you up?'

'The farmer's wife.'

'The farmer's wife? So she's your mother.'

'I thought she was,' said Omelette. 'But I've changed my mind. I saw somebody else I thought could be my mother.'

'Oh, who would that be?' asked the fat hen, who was finding it difficult to keep her face straight.

Omelette tried hard to remember what the farmer's wife had called the handsome creature who had chased all the hens, but he couldn't, so he tried to describe Eric. 'Well, it was not as big as the horse and not as small as you. It had horns and a white beard and it was extremely handsome.'

They looked at one another puzzled, murmuring amongst themselves. 'Horns and a beard?'

'I know who it is,' said a pretty hen. 'It's Eric.'

5

'Is it?' said Omelette. 'Well, that's what I'm going to be when I grow up, An Eric.'

'An Eric!' The turkey ran in circles with tears pouring down her face while the two ducks just lay on their backs in the dust, beaks gasping for breath, their wings spread, their cream stomachs heaving.

'Ladies,' said the fat hen, 'ladies! Please!' She turned to Omelette. 'You do know that it's *Eric*, not *an* Eric, and he's a goat.'

'Well, that's what I'm going to be when I grow up,' said Omelette.

'I don't think I've ever seen a goat with a beak and feathers before,' said the turkey.

A large goose sidled up to him. She looked about her as though she was worried someone might be listening. She leaned towards Omelette, and whispered huskily out of the corner of her beak. 'And have you thanked your mother properly?' she asked.

Omelette shook his head.

'You haven't?' said the goose in astonishment. She shook her head. 'Oh dear,' she said sadly.

'Oh dear, oh dear,' murmured the rest disapprovingly.

Omelette was alarmed. 'Is that bad?'

'Bad! Is that bad! He wants to know if it's bad. Of course it's bad. It's just about the baddest thing there is.'

'But what can I do?' asked Omelette. He was close to tears. 'Couldn't I go now and thank her right away?'

'I think it might be best,' replied the fat hen with the utmost gravity. 'Follow me.'

She strode across the farmyard with Omelette scurrying behind her. The others followed chuckling amongst themselves. It was the best joke they'd played in years. They couldn't wait to see the expression on the goat's face when the little bantam thanked him for being his mother. Whenever Omelette looked around they looked as serious as they could.

The procession marched past the pig sty. Enoch, the Staffordshire boar, stuck his snout over the wall.

Omelette asked him, 'Have you seen goat Eric, my mother?'

'Oh ah,' said Enoch. He scratched behind his ear. 'Last time I saw Eric he was eating windfalls in the orchard,' and he pointed.

They all marched away in the direction of the orchard.

Doris, Enoch's wife, came out, 'Here, Enoch, why is all them hens a followin' that little bantam?'

'He's looking for his ma, Doris my love.'

'Who's his ma then, Enoch?'

'Eric.'

'Eric! He's a goat.'

'I know that.'

'Goats don't have chicks, do they, Enoch?'

'Not as I heard tell.' Enoch paused. 'Know what I think, gal? I think them hens is a pulling of that little bantam's leg; both of 'em.'

Two

That morning Eric was feeling particularly bad tempered. It was extremely hot and the bees and flies were bothering him a good deal.

'Blasted flies,' he grumbled to himself, swishing his tail. 'Blasted bees,' he cursed, shaking his head. Deep down, Eric wasn't really so disagreeable. It was just that he was a bit lonely. He didn't like being alone. It made him grumpy. Some days when the flies or the bees or the hornets bothered him the slightest thing would make him angry. Then he would take it out on the hens. He didn't know why he hated hens so much. Perhaps it was the way they fussed and gossiped. Most of the time they gave him a wide berth, but on those days when they came too close he would lower his horns and chase them across the farm. It seemed to make him feel better.

The procession climbed up the hill with Omelette in their midst. When they saw Eric they stopped and crouched behind a low bush at a safe distance. The fat hen pointed at the distant Eric. 'There's your mother,' she said.

Omelette saw the goat, his head in the long grass, chewing the windfalls.

'Oh my goodness,' he murmured in wonder. 'Goat Eric, my mother!' He turned to the fat hen. 'I wonder if you could give me a few hints on . . . er . . .'

'How to greet a mother?'

'Yes, I don't know how to go about it. I don't want to mess it up.'

'Of course not.' The fat hen looked at him solemnly. 'If I were you I should proceed as follows. Creep up quietly, cough discreetly, then when she sees you, say very softly "Mummy" and throw yourself into her arms.'

Omelette drew himself up and took a deep breath. 'Right,' he said.

The fat hen patted him on the back. 'Off you go,' she said. 'And good luck.'

Omelette marched across the meadow. 'Ahem.' He coughed politely.

'Blasted hornets,' murmured Eric and continued munching. Omelette coughed once more only louder.

Eric turned. He saw a small feathered creature staring up at him, his eyes gleaming with admiration. He knew it was a chick of some sort but he couldn't be sure. He had never seen a bantam before. For a minute the two stared at one another.

Omelette looked up into Eric's fine yellow eyes. He swallowed, took a deep breath, whispered 'Mummy', and at the same time flung himself headlong into the arms of the surprised goat.

It was the first time Eric had been embraced by a bantam chick. It took him by surprise, and, thinking that he was being attacked, he shook his head violently and Omelette flew gently through the air and landed head first in the duck pond.

Behind the hedge the watchers clutched themselves for joy. The fat hen said, 'Mother' and threw herself laughing on a small duck.

'Ssh!' said the turkey.

9

Omelette struggled up the bank. It wasn't the response that he had expected from his mother.

Eric was eating once more. He still felt angry. Usually when he chased the hens he felt better, but his tussle with the little bantam worried him. Actually he felt a little ashamed of himself. The bantam was rather too small to be a worthy opponent and there had been something about him. He spotted a particularly succulent apple and began chewing.

Behind him he heard a rather damp cough, followed by a timid, 'Excuse me.'

He looked round. A drenched and bedraggled chicken stared up at him. There was duckweed on his head.

'Excuse me,' he said, 'but *are* you?'

'Am I what?'

'My mother, of course.'

'Look,' said Eric very slowly and clearly, 'I am a goat. Although a little past my prime I am still thought handsome. My family have lived hereabouts for sixteen hundred years. I am intelligent and brave. I have four legs and magnificent horns, a fine beard and I butt things. Especially things that annoy me. That proves I'm a goat. You, on the other hand, are a species of fowl. You are extremely small, with two legs, feathers and, like most fowl, you are of limited intelligence. I could not possibly be your mother. What is more I am a *he*. He's are not mothers. And especially they are not the mothers of wet little fowl like you. Do you understand? For the last time I am not your mother. Not, not, not! Now, unless you want to go for another swim, buzz off for ever and leave me in peace.'

And with that he strode away.

Omelette, sadly, watched him retreating.

'But,' Omelette called after him, 'you must be my mother. The hens told me.'

'Hens!' snorted Eric. 'What hens?'

Omelette pointed to the bush.

'So the hens put you up to this, did they? I might have known.'

His eyes blazed and he strode over to the bush and stared at it very hard. 'Are there any hens behind there?' he demanded threateningly.

'No,' said one particularly dim chicken. The bush began to tremble.

Eric raised himself on his back legs.

'Charge!' he roared and raced at the bush. The hens emerged in a flood of brown feathers. 'Tut-tut,' they said to one another as they raced away as swiftly as legs and wings would carry them in the direction of the farmyard. Eric flung himself after them.

Omelette followed him at a safe distance. Eric looked round at him threateningly. Omelette stopped. But as soon as Eric began to walk on again, Omelette followed. In the pig sty, Enoch was sniffing the air and gazing at nothing in particular.

'Morning,' said Eric.

'Ah,' said Enoch.

'Blasted fowl,' said Eric, 'keeps following me.'

'Fowl. Ah,' said Enoch.

Omelette walked past the sty. Enoch looked at him curiously.

'I'm a goat,' said Omelette. He nodded after Eric. 'That's my mother.'

Enoch shook his head, 'Oh ah,' he said. It was best not to get involved in the squabbles of other families. 'Ah,' he said again.

He wondered if he'd said too much.

Eric paused in the shelter of the barn and looked around. Seeing Omelette gazing fondly at him, and beginning to feel desperate, Eric put on the most threatening glare he could muster. 'Look here,' he said, 'I've warned you. You call me mother once more and it will be the worse for you.'

'But you *are* my mother.'

'I AM NOT YOUR MOTHER!' shouted the exasperated Eric. 'And you're not a goat.'

'Am a goat,' said Omelette.

'Not,' said Eric.

'Am!' said Omelette.

'NOT!' shouted Eric in such a loud voice that it made Omelette blink and step back a few paces. 'Not, not, not!'

'Why?' asked Omelette.

Eric furrowed his brow and sighed. 'I don't know,' he said in exasperation. 'You just aren't, that's all.'

'Why?' repeated Omelette.

Eric groaned and thought about it. 'Well,' he said, 'for one thing goats butt.' It wasn't much but it was all he could think of.

'I butt,' said Omelette simply. 'Watch!'

He lowered his head, 'Charge,' he shouted, and head down, scampered across the farmyard. He couldn't see very well. He began running round in circles and only stopped when he ran his head into the haystack. He struggled out and walked over to Eric.

'See,' he said, 'I butt.' He grinned proudly. There were bits of straw in his feathers.

Eric sighed. 'It doesn't mean a thing,' he said. 'Goats kick.'

He turned his back on a low stone wall and let fly with both hooves. The wall crumbled. A couple of angry hornets flew out and into the barn. Eric walked over to Omelette and whispered in his ear. 'I'm not really a violent sort of creature. It's live and let live, as far as I'm concerned. But if you don't leave me alone you'll end up like that wall.'

Omelette gazed at the scattered stones. Young as he was Omelette knew when he was being challenged.

'I can kick,' he said brightly.

He strode up to the barn door, turned his back on it, lifted both legs at the same time and fell flat on his face, stunning himself.

'See,' said Eric. 'Now, go away, you ugly little feathered monster. I don't want you. Go away and leave me in peace.' And he strode into the barn slamming the door shut behind him. He slumped down, his body against it. He had never felt so depressed in his whole life. The other farm animals drifted away. The fun seemed to be over.

13

Omelette walked over to the barn door. He leaned his weight against it. It wouldn't open.

Omelette scratched at the door but he couldn't get it to shift. He sat down in the dust. It was awful not to be wanted by your own mother. He wondered if he should go back to the farmer's wife. But she had shut him out as well. Nobody seemed to want him.

An angry hornet buzzed past his nose and then settled on his head. Omelette didn't care. For the first time in his young life he knew what it was to be alone. He settled himself down on the ground. The hornet flew away into the barn through a chink in the door.

'Even the hornet doesn't want me,' thought Omelette sadly.

The fat hen and the turkey walked past. They pointed and giggled.

Omelette felt too sad to chase them. He didn't feel that he would ever move again.

Three

Omelette closed his eyes and shuffled sadly in the dust. He would wait outside the barn until Eric came out. He would wait for ever; until he died, if necessary. Then Eric would be sorry. He began to daydream. He saw Eric standing beside a mound of earth. On the top was a simple wooden cross. On the cross was written, 'Poor Omelette Who Never Had A Mother'.

A terrible squeal woke him. Then another and another. They were coming from inside the barn. Wood splintered. Glass broke.

'Eric must be in trouble,' thought Omelette. 'I must help him.'

He pushed against the barn door. It opened a crack and Omelette crept through. The screams had stopped. In the gloom Omelette heard a soft moaning. He peered into the darkness. Beams of light slanted down from the high windows. Through the dust Omelette saw a white shape. Eric was standing still by the wall. His head was twisted over his shoulder and he was chewing something on his back. He groaned with anger and annoyance. Omelette wondered if it was his fault.

'You do seem to be upset,' said Omelette sympathetically.

'Upset,' shouted Eric, 'of course I'm upset, you stupid fowl. You'd be upset if you had a hornet sting in your back.'

And he twisted his head round and began chewing once more.

'Just stay still for a moment,' said Omelette, 'and I'll see if I can get it out. Beaks are very useful for that sort of thing.'

He fluttered down on to the goat's back. There, protruding from the white goat hair beside the bumpy ridge of his spine was the hornet's sting. It looked like a particularly long thorn. Omelette grasped it with his beak.

'If this hurts you'll be for it,' said Eric. He closed his eyes and braced himself.

Omelette gave a swift tug and the sting came out cleanly. He showed it to Eric who inspected it carefully. 'To think that something so little could give so much pain.'

'Well, it's out now,' said Omelette.

Eric was embarrassed. He was grateful to the little bantam but didn't want to encourage him. He mumbled a few words indistinctly into his beard. Most of what he said Omelette found difficult to hear. But there were a few words like 'sorry' and 'bit short' and 'rather hasty'. Eric wasn't used to apologising, especially to bantams. Somehow Omelette understood this.

'I understand, Mum,' he said.

At the word 'mum' Eric turned his back and raised his hooves to kick Omelette. Then he hesitated. How ungrateful to kick someone who had helped him. Omelette was cowering behind a piece of broken mirror. 'I am not your mum – I mean mother, and you are not a goat.'

'Am a goat,' said Omelette defiantly.

Eric sighed. He walked up and down thinking. The broken mirror caught his eye. 'Come with me,' he said.

He pointed at the mirror. 'Have a look at yourself.'

Omelette walked up to the mirror and pressed his beak against the glass.

'It's yourself you can see in the glass,' said Eric.

Omelette stared into the mirror.

'Myself?' said Omelette in dismay. 'You mean that's what I look like.'

Eric nodded.

'But I haven't got any horns or a beard. That can't be me.'

'That's you, all right,' said Eric.

For a few seconds Omelette looked at himself in silence. The other chicken that he knew was himself, stared back. How sad he looks, thought Omelette. Then he cheered up.

'Perhaps it's only temporary,' he said. 'In a few months or years I'll start looking like a goat, won't I?'

Eric shook his head. 'I'm afraid not,' he said.

Omelette walked away. He looked back over his shoulder. He couldn't help thinking he looked even more ridiculous from the back than he did from the front; like a hen gone wrong.

Eric sat down facing him and tried to explain very clearly.

'Let me tell you some of the facts of life. Goats are goats and bantams are bantams. That's the way the world is and nothing can change it,' said Eric.

'Not ever?' said Omelette sadly.

'Not ever,' said Eric.

'D'you mean I'm always going to look like this?'

'I'm afraid so,' said Eric.

A tear trickled down Omelette's cheek.

Eric watched it. The strangest feeling swept over him. 'Now look here, old chap, it's no good moping and feeling

17

sorry for yourself. There are worse things than being a bantam, you know.'

Omelette stared at his reflection. 'Like what?' he said.

Eric frowned. 'Like lots of things. Like for example . . . er . . .'

He thought hard but nothing would come into his head, 'Oh, lots of things. More than I can be bothered to mention.' He smiled, trying to cheer Omelette up. But Omelette's spirits were not to be raised.

'I hate myself,' he said. 'I wish I was dead.' He kicked moodily at the straw. 'I look ridiculous and on top of everything I haven't got a mother.' He looked up at Eric plaintively, 'Unless you'd like to . . .'

Eric shook his head.

'I understand,' he said. 'Sorry I was such a nuisance. I won't bother you again.'

And he turned and walked out of the barn across the farmyard. His shoulders sagged and his feet dragged in the dust. 'Everybody has a mother except me,' he said mournfully to himself.

At the edge of the farm by a broken fence was an empty oil drum. He squeezed himself inside and crouched in the dark corner. Nobody would find him there. 'This is where I will die,' he murmured sadly to himself. He wondered how long it took to die. It was getting darker and a wind sprang up. Omelette fell asleep.

He was awoken by a snuffling noise.

'Hello,' said a voice.

Omelette said nothing.

'Anybody there?' said the voice, knocking on the drum.

'No,' said Omelette. 'Go away!'

'Ah! Been looking for you all over, old chap.'

Omelette recognised Eric's voice.

'Go away,' repeated Omelette.

'Up to anything interesting in there?'

'I'm busy,' said Omelette.

'Doing what?' asked Eric.

'Dying,' said Omelette.

'Oh, I see,' said Eric, 'that must be jolly hard work. I'll leave you then. Pity really. It's a beautiful evening. I was going for a little stroll.'

With a certain longing Omelette thought about the sky, the hills and the river. But he said nothing.

'You know,' said Eric. 'I felt like you once. Want to hear about it?'

It surprised Omelette that Eric should ever have wished to die too. He felt very curious.

'Want to hear about it?' repeated Eric.

'No,' said Omelette.

'You could die afterwards. Just a little stroll, then we'll come back and you can carry on with your dying.'

Omelette hesitated. 'Oh, all right,' he said grudgingly.

He scrambled out of the oil drum. The brightness of the setting sun glinted in his eyes.

'Thought we'd walk along the top of the hill and look at the river.'

And Eric marched off at a brisk pace with Omelette having to trot to keep up. At last he stopped and gazed at the fiery red of the sky, humming softly to himself.

Omelette wanted to hear Eric's story but didn't like to ask. They walked back to the oil drum.

Omelette coughed. 'Think I'll carry on dying now,' he said.

'Fair enough,' said Eric. ''Bye.' He began to walk away. 'Charming evening,' Omelette heard him murmur.

Omelette could contain his curiosity no longer. ''Scuse me,' he called, 'weren't you going to tell me something?'

Eric stopped, 'Tell you. . . ?'

'You know, about dying. You were unhappy once, wanted to die.'

'Oh that,' said Eric, 'you wouldn't be interested in all that.'

'Yes, I would,' said Omelette.

They took another turn about the meadow before Eric paused and then began to speak very seriously, gazing over the valley. Omelette did the same.

'When I first came here I had my whole family with me. Wife, children, cousins. That sort of thing. Happy days. Couple of years ago the Westmorelands were short of money. Sold all my family to another farmer. Left me on my own. Hated it. Thoroughly miserable. I stopped eating. I thought I'd just lie down on the ground and die.

Westmoreland didn't know what to do. Sent for the vet. Nothing wrong with me, he said. Trouble was inside. Broken heart, you see. You can die of it.'

Omelette nodded. He knew all about that.

'Then,' continued Eric, 'one day when I had hardly the strength to lift my head, quite suddenly two thoughts came into my mind. It was a beautiful evening like tonight. And I thought to myself: If I die I shall never see another sunset like that ever again. Seemed a shame.'

Omelette gazed at the red sky reflected in the river. The idea of dying seemed to be fading away. He looked up at Eric who was looking particularly noble.

'What was the second thing?' he asked.

'Ah,' murmured Eric. 'I thought perhaps one day I might meet a friend; that I wouldn't be alone any more. I thought what a shame it would be if this friend should turn up and I wasn't there to know them.'

'Because you'd be dead.'

'Exactly. What a waste that would be.' Eric paused once more.

Omelette wondered if that was the end of the story.

'And did you ever meet that friend?' he asked hesitantly.

'Oh yes. Yes, I did.'

'When was that?'

'Today.'

'Today,' said Omelette. He felt rather jealous. 'Who is it? How did you meet him?'

'At first I didn't like him very much. But then he did something for me.'

'What was that?' Omelette wondered.

'I got stung by a hornet and he took the sting out.'

Omelette stopped and gazed up at him. 'You mean your friend is . . . Me!' said Omelette.

21

'If that's all right?'

'All right,' said Omelette. 'But I thought . . .'

'I can't be your mother, mind. But there's nothing to stop us being friends, is there?'

'Friends,' said Omelette. It seemed to him like the most wonderful word he had ever heard. He whispered it aloud. Then he hesitated. 'But you're ashamed of me,' said Omelette. 'You said they'd all make fun of you. You'd be a laughing stock.'

By this time they were back at the oil drum. One or two hens pecked at the seeds in the grass.

The hens had spotted them. 'There's that Omelette with his mother.' They began to cackle raucously.

'Ashamed of you?' said Eric. 'Not a bit of it.' He nodded at the hens. 'Think we've got time for a little charge before you die?' asked Eric.

Omelette nodded.

'Then hop on board,' said Eric.

Omelette leapt on to his back. The hens laughed louder.

'Charge!' said Eric.

'Charge!' shouted Omelette, and together they galloped across the grass scattering the hens to the four winds.

'Well, I suppose I'd better leave you to get on with your dying,' said Eric.

'Dying! Well, I thought I'd leave it for a bit.'

Eric nodded. He walked past the farmhouse with Omelette still on his back. The farmer and his wife were sitting on the slate porch.

'Just look at that,' said Mrs Westmoreland. 'Our Omelette hitching a ride. Like a bareback rider in the circus.'

Her husband rubbed his eyes in amazement. 'It's all

that milk you give him. Reckon you spoiled him something rotten. I always said he'd get above himself.'

'He's above himself now, all right,' said his wife.

Eric had a small stone house to himself by the barn. There was straw on the floor. Eric made himself comfortable whilst Omelette crouched in the rafters.

'Keep your eyes peeled. You see anything, let me know,' said Eric and fell asleep instantly.

Omelette was tired. He went over everything that had happened to him during the day. He was disappointed about not having a mother but he had a friend and he had a home. On his first day in the huge world he felt he had lived a lifetime. Sometimes he snoozed but mostly he stayed awake. After all it was his job to guard Eric.

He scanned the horizon. What was that monstrous thing? It lifted itself out of the hillside, round and huge and red sending long rods of pink and white sliding across the countryside towards him. Omelette's heart filled with fear. In his fear he cried out.

'Cocoricooooooo,' he crowed in a cracked voice.

Eric woke with a start.

'What is it? What's happening?'

'There! Look there! The monster, the monster is coming,' screamed Omelette.

Eric peered in the direction Omelette was pointing. Then he began to laugh.

'Monster!' he exclaimed. 'That's no monster, that's the sun.'

Later Omelette fell asleep. Sometimes he woke up and saw Eric calmly cropping the grasses. The sun was high.

'That's my friend,' Omelette said to no one in particular. 'My friend.'

And then he slipped back once more into that contented darkness that people call sleep.

Four

From then on Eric and Omelette were never out of each other's company. Omelette was as happy as the day was long. Each day he grew a little larger and his feathers changed colour from a dull brown to green and red and blue. Autumn grew into winter and then into early spring. During the long afternoons the two friends would lie in the long grass of the orchard talking of this and that. Usually Omelette asked questions which the wise goat would try to answer. One afternoon Omelette remembered something the farmer's wife had said that had been worrying him for some time.

'Eric,' he said, 'tell me about Happy Christmas?'

'Happy Christmas? Oh, you mean Christmas. That's to do with snow, and everybody being very happy and eating a great deal.'

'Is that what being happy means?'

'It does for humans,' said Eric, nodding his head, 'but on the other farm it wasn't always happy for the turkeys and the geese and the hens.'

'Why?'

Eric hesitated. 'Well, they sort of disappeared.'

'Disappeared?'

'Yes. Never to be seen again.'

'Does that mean I'll disappear at Christmas?'

'No,' said Eric. 'Not on this farm. We're all pets here.'

25

'Yes,' said Omelette. 'I like it here. How will I know when Christmas is near? So that I can hide. Just to be on the safe side.'

Eric laughed. 'You'll know all right. It will get cold and sometimes there'll be snow.'

'Snow?' said Omelette.

'White bits come out of the sky,' explained Eric, 'and everybody gets excited.'

'Except for the hens and ducks and geese,' said Omelette.

'Ah yes, except for them,' said Eric.

After that, Omelette kept an anxious eye on the sky. At the first sign of anything white falling out of it he would run for his oil drum and hide until it was all over.

One afternoon Eric woke and couldn't find his friend. He searched everywhere, but he was nowhere to be found. As he was taking his evening stroll about the orchard he heard strange noises coming from the oil drum. He approached it tentatively.

'Anybody there?' he asked.

'Friend or foe? Are you white and have you just fallen out of the sky?' said Omelette.

'It's me — Eric. What are you doing in there?'

'Hiding,' said Omelette.

'Hiding?'

'Yes,' said Omelette. 'So that I won't disappear.'

'Why should you disappear?'

'Because it's Christmas.'

'Christmas!' snorted Eric. 'How can it be Christmas? It's the middle of April.'

'No, it isn't,' said Omelette, 'it's Christmas. I know because the white things came out of the sky.'

'Where?' asked Eric. 'Show me.'

'Is it safe to come out?' said Omelette, emerging from

the darkness of the oil drum. He led the way across the orchard to a cherry tree. He pointed to the floor. 'Look at all the snow,' he said.

Eric began to laugh. 'That's not snow,' he said. 'That's blossom falling off the cherry tree. Look,' said Eric and he shook the tree. White blossom fluttered down covering both of them.

Omelette heaved a sigh of relief. 'It's not snow, it's blossom,' he sang, hurling the white petals into the air and dancing up and down. 'Blossom, blossom, blossom.'

The days passed, one very much like another. Omelette greeted each new day by standing on the stone wall and singing to the sun at the top of his voice. To be honest his voice wasn't very beautiful, in fact it was rather tuneless, but it carried well and woke the farmer at the right time.

And after Omelette had finished his morning song the two friends would stroll about the farm talking, which usually meant Omelette asking a lot of questions and Eric trying to answer them. And when they'd finished talking, Omelette would leap on to Eric's back and they'd chase the hens together.

But then one evening, a month later, while the farmer and his wife were visiting their daughter, Jenny, at her farm on the other side of the valley, out of the gloom of the night the enemy came and everything changed.

Five

As soon as Omelette saw the two men approaching the farm he sensed something was wrong. Most visitors spoke loudly and walked straight up to the door. These two, on the other hand, walked silently and looked about them furtively. They carried a long net and large sticks in their hands. Involuntarily a cry of warning rose to Omelette's throat. But the hens ignored him.

'Oh shut up!' they cried. 'Don't you know it's bedtime.'

'Don't say I didn't warn you,' he muttered and went off to consult Eric.

The men drove their van up to the pig sty, blocking off the exits and trapping the sheep who were being kept in the lower pastures. They turned off the headlights of the van and worked with torches in the moonlight. One of them opened the rear doors to the van and lowered the tail gate. First they herded the sheep into the van and then the pigs. Enoch tried to turn back but the men shouted and struck him with their clubs. He squealed in terror. Omelette felt afraid. He looked round for Eric. *He* would know what to do. But Eric was nowhere to be seen.

Omelette crouched quaking in the shelter of a low hedge. He watched in horror as the two men rounded up as many of the farm animals as they could lay hands on. They worked with a quiet frenzy talking to each other only

29

when they had to and then in hoarse whispers. After half an hour they stopped. They stood looking about them.

'Here, hadn't we better be off, Harry?'

'You scared of the dark or sumfink?' said Harry.

'Ain't scared of nuffink, Harry. Just thinking about the geezer who lives here. Don't want them coming back and catching us.'

'Snouty, you make me sick. You're so yellow.' He wiped his hands. 'All right, let's get movin', we don't want . . .'

He didn't get a chance to finish his sentence. There was a thunder of hooves and suddenly he was struck by a pair of sharp horns and sent sprawling in the mud.

'Eric!' whispered Omelette. His eyes glowed with pride. Only Eric would have the courage to do that.

'What the . . .' shouted Harry. He tried to get to his feet but Eric was at him again, bowling him over and over.

'Get him off me. Get him off me.' The man called Snout threw a net over both figures, then began clubbing at random.

'Ouch,' screamed Harry. 'Not me. Don't hit me, you stupid berk. Hit the goat.'

Eventually Harry managed to get clear of the net and they bundled Eric still bucking and rearing and entangled into the back of the van. Omelette could restrain himself no longer. He couldn't leave Eric to fight this battle alone. He half ran, half flew, across the darkness of the farmyard and threw himself on the man called Snout and scratched with abandoned fury.

Snout roared, and beat at Omelette – who felt himself tumbling across the floor, a dull pain in his side. He shook himself and returned to the fray. But he felt a powerful hand grip him tightly around the throat.

'Gotcha!' cried Harry in triumph.

30

Omelette turned his head this way and that, but could not free himself from the iron grip. He opened his beak for air, but his throat was held too tightly. He felt himself growing faint. The man called Harry leaned his face towards him. On his left cheek, just beneath his eye, was a small tattoo. It showed two knives crossed.

'Think you could beat Harry did you, you midget?' he sneered. 'You wait 'til Christmas comes and I'll have you special just for meself.' Omelette struck his beak at the tattoo.

'Aaaaaah!' Harry screamed, clutching his hand to his face. He flung the little bantam into the back of the van with the other animals. The doors smashed shut. Then the engine started and they were rolling towards the gate.

What pandemonium and terror there was within the van! The hens and ducks flew into each other and into the walls of the vehicle in a blind panic as it raced bouncing and lurching down the rutted track.

'Why did you come back?' asked Eric above the din.

'I couldn't leave you to fight those men on your own,' replied Omelette hoarsely. His neck was still sore.

'Not very sensible. Now we're both caught,' said Eric. He noticed the little bantam's expression. 'But I appreciate the loyalty,' he said in a softer tone.

'Where do you think they're taking us?'

'Can't you smell it?' said Eric.

'Smell what?' Omelette lifted his beak and sniffed the air. There was the strangest scent. He couldn't put a name to it but it filled him with a strange, nameless fear.

'What is it?'

'Blood,' said Eric. He looked about him and whispered. 'I've smelled it before on the other farm. It means that they're taking us to the slaughterhouse.'

31

'Slaughter . . .' cried Omelette.

'Ssh,' hissed Eric.

But it was too late, the other creatures had heard the word. It passed amongst them like wild fire, and the panic increased and became hysteria.

'What can we do?' asked Omelette.

'Well, I'd rather die fighting,' said Eric. He raised his voice above the screaming and lamentation. 'Make way there. Give me room.' He cleared a corridor down the centre of the van. 'Away from the door there,' he ordered. The animals moved.

'What are you going to do?' asked Omelette.

'They'll have to stop somewhere. If I can kick this door open, follow me. Come out fighting and then run for your life.'

But it was late at night and the roads were empty. The van moved through the gloom for mile upon mile never having to stop. The animals stared at one another dismally. Then, at last, the van slowed and finally stopped. The man called Stout climbed down. A small tree had fallen across the lane.

'I'll shift it,' Snout called to his companion.

Eric braced himself. 'Ready?' he asked.

Omelette nodded his head determinedly. 'Ready,' he said.

Eric turned his back on the door. For a second he was silent and still. Then with a sudden cry he lifted his back legs and crashed his hooves into the door. One door splintered, but the rest held.

'What's that?' said Snout.

'That blasted goat,' said Harry. 'He's trying to break the door down.'

He picked up a shotgun that lay on hooks behind his

head. 'Might as well kill him here as wait for the slaughterhouse.' And he laughed softly.

He walked round to the rear of the van. Snout followed him.

Crash! Eric's hooves struck once more. The door gave. But it was still held by the chain.

'Help, murder,' screamed the geese and flew wildly from side to side. Their white feathers filled the van. Eric panted with exhaustion. He'd put everything he had into those two wild kicks. His rear leg was bleeding just above the right hoof where it had struck the iron bolt.

Through the chink in the door they could see the two men. The man called Harry pushed a cartridge into his shotgun. Eric's eyes were closed as he gathered every ounce of his remaining strength, then charged headlong at the chain. With a splintering roar the door swung open knocking the two men to the ground. Eric picked himself up.

'Liberty!' he shouted and his voice echoed off the hills and the stones. 'Come on.'

Omelette scrambled on to Eric's back.

'Charge!' shouted Omelette.

'Charge!' shouted Eric and leapt out into the night. The two men were just climbing to their feet when the enraged goat with the bantam cock on his back arched through the air towards them. They just had time to take in this vision before Eric struck them with the full force of his powerful horns and they were once more rolling and grovelling in the mud.

The other animals piled out of the van. Enoch, the boar, leapt out, landing on Snout's stomach and knocking all the breath out of him. The hens and sheep and ducks and goats followed, filling the roadway. A car came down the

road, the driver slammed on his brakes and skidded sideways into the van.

Eric was plunging down the hillside towards the safety of the woodland with Omelette swaying and bobbing on his back. The bantam heard a shout behind him and looked back to see Harry with the shotgun to his shoulder.

'You wait,' he screamed in fury. 'If I catch you, killing'll be too good. I'll have your guts for catapults.'

There was a flash of fire followed by a crack. Omelette ducked his head. He felt a rush of wind and a branch just above his head exploded in a puff of smoke before crashing down. And then they were in the forest. The branches of the trees lashed and clutched at them. He pressed himself flat to Eric's back. He could hear his panting breath and the racing of the blood through his veins. As Eric swung and dodged between the trees it took all Omelette's skill and concentration to hang on. He could still hear Harry's voice screaming threats but it was further off now. And then it was gone altogether and there was only the sound of Eric's pounding hooves and the cracking and splintering of the occasional branch. Mile upon mile they ran until they reached the very heart of the forest. Then, when he could run no more, Eric stopped. For a time he merely stood in the forest clearing without the strength to move. His head hung low and his sides rose and fell convulsively as he gasped for air. Then he lay down unable to speak.

Omelette watched him for a little while. An owl hooted ominously. Somewhere in the darkness he heard a twig crack. Then silence. He had the feeling that a hundred unseen eyes were watching them, and he shivered. How glad he was that he wasn't on his own. He gazed fondly at Eric, whose eyes were closed.

'How lucky I am,' thought Omelette, 'to have someone as strong and fearless as Eric for a friend. If it hadn't been for him I'd be on my way to the slaughterhouse by now. I might even be dead already. Hanging upside down on a hook.' He shivered and wondered what it was like to be dead. The thought was too big for him. He would ask Eric about that. Later. Perhaps tomorrow when he was feeling stronger. Then he thought about all the other animals and was downcast once more.

Eric was sleeping easily now. Eric had done his part. Now it was his turn. He peered out into the forest. Around him the creatures of the night began to emerge. Omelette marched slowly round the form of his sleeping friend. He felt much older. He sat down on the ground and peered about him. But no matter how hard he tried to stay alert his eyelids kept closing. The air became cold. He huddled closer to Eric who half-woke for a second but then turned over. He mumbled something in his sleep. Omelette wondered what it was. He laid his ear closer.

'Liberty!' said Eric softly. 'Liberty!' His feet moved jerkily in his sleep.

Despite the pain in his wing and side Omelette could not help smiling, 'Liberty!' he repeated softly, before he, too, fell into a deep sleep.

Six

The sun was already high in the sky when Omelette awoke. It wasn't like him to sleep late. He looked about him. Where could he be? Where was the farmhouse with all its familiar sounds? The snort of the pigs, the querulous hens and the cackling ducks? And the sunlight was thinner as it filtered through tall, dark trees. Where was he? Then slowly the terrible events of the previous day came creeping back into his mind. Had all that really happened? Surely it had been one of his dreams. Then he noticed the trail of blood on the forest floor. No, it hadn't been a dream. He shivered in fear.

Eric? Where was Eric? He searched about him. The forest glade was empty. Yet he had a feeling that someone was watching him. Somewhere out there in the shadows of the trees he sensed a pair of eyes. He glared about him with his fiercest expression but his heart was thumping with fear. In the air was a sharp, bitter stench that he had never smelled before. And yet it seemed to carry a message to him and the message was 'Enemy'. He was just about to cry out in fear and alarm when something touched him on the shoulder.

'Wouldn't do that if I was you,' said a voice at his shoulder.

Omelette gasped and looked around. It was Eric. He breathed a sigh of relief.

'Wouldn't do that just now,' repeated Eric. 'We don't know who or what's out there. The fewer that know we're here, the better. Those men might still be about. We don't want them to know where we are.'

Omelette nodded. Not for the first time he acknowledged how fortunate he was to have such a wise and experienced friend as Eric to accompany him.

'It was just that I smelled something. There was something out there.'

'Probably a fox. Wouldn't bother me of course, but he'd snap your head off as soon as look at you.'

Omelette gulped and moved closer to his companion.

'Don't worry,' said Eric, 'he won't bother you with me around. Come on.'

He set off through the forest with Omelette trotting behind.

'Where are we going?' he asked. 'What shall we do?'

'First thing is to get out of this forest. If I can find a few landmarks, the river for example, we might know where we are. Then we can decide what's best to do.'

'Couldn't we go back to the farm?' asked Omelette.

Eric pushed his way through some thick undergrowth.

'That's what we have to do if we can ever find it,' he replied. He stopped and looked at Omelette. The little bantam had his back legs caught in some brambles. He tugged. The brambles suddenly released him and he fell flat on his face. He climbed to his feet. There was mud on his feathers and in his eyes and his wing hurt.

'Will we be home soon, Eric?'

'I don't know.'

'How far is it, Eric?'

'I don't know.'

'How long will it take?'

'How should I know?'

'Eric, I'm hungry. When can we eat?'

Eric stopped. 'Look, stop asking so many questions. What we must do is just keep going. Get out of this forest. Then we'll see.'

Omelette looked up at his friend. 'Am I being a nuisance, Eric?'

'Just don't talk so much. Try to think a bit before you speak.'

Eric was walking quickly. Omelette ran alongside him trying to keep pace and gazing up.

'Think?' he said. There was mud in his eyes. It was difficult to see. He tripped over a low branch.

'Yes, think,' said Eric. He waited for Omelette to catch up. 'And when you've thought of something sensible, say it. But not until then.'

And Eric marched onwards at an even swifter pace whistling a military tune.

This was obviously the thing to do when hiking adventurously through a forest. Omelette joined in on the whistling as best he could. He tried to keep step but his little legs had to move at three times the pace of Eric's. It was hard to run and whistle at the same time.

'If you're going to whistle, then kindly try to keep in tune,' said Eric without looking at him. 'Or else sing your own tune.'

Omelette didn't really know any tunes. He looked about him for inspiration.

Eric stopped suddenly. He stared at something on the ground. Omelette joined him.

'Look!' said Eric. Omelette looked. All he could see was a soft patch of mud with some marks scratched into it.

'What is . . .' he began.

'Think,' said Eric sharply.

Omelette put on a thinking expression. It didn't help.

'What d'you see?' asked Eric patiently.

'Mud.'

'What else?'

'Marks.'

'What marks?'

Omelette looked closer. He had a flash of inspiration, 'Claw marks.'

'Whose?'

'Er, hens.' Omelette smiled. His thinking hadn't been in vain. Then he had another thought. 'That means hens must have been here.' He felt proud of his detective work.

'Put your foot in them,' said Eric.

Carefully Omelette placed his claw in the marks. They matched perfectly.

'The hen must be the same size as me,' he said. 'What a coincidence.'

Eric sighed. 'Of course they're the same size.' Eric sighed again. 'Look around; recognise that tree, that bush? Those are your footprints. We're back where we started. We've gone round in a circle.'

Omelette felt a great gloom descending on him. Round in a circle? Perhaps they would never get home. Everywhere in the forest looked just the same as everywhere else. What if they never found their way out. Suddenly he began to feel hungry and bad tempered.

'Hate this forest,' he grumbled. 'Hate the dark. Fed up. Want to die. Want to die now. NOW!' He stamped his feet in a tantrum.

Eric looked at him.

'You want to die, eh?' he said. 'Fine.'

He looked about him. 'Well, this looks as good a place as any. First-rate place for dying, I should say. Happy dying. Goodbye,' and he strode away whistling into the gloom. Omelette ran after him.

'Eric, where are you going? You can't leave me,' he screamed.

Eric looked down at the little bantam.

'But I thought you wanted to give up and die. So I thought I'd let you get on with it. Chin chin.' And he began to walk off again.

Once more Omelette caught him up.

'But what about me? Don't leave me Eric, please. Please take me with you. Please!'

Eric looked him straight in the eye. 'If you want to come with me there are certain conditions. You mustn't grumble or sulk or talk about dying. Do you understand?'

Omelette nodded. 'I understand,' he said.

41

'You must be cheerful in the face of danger. And when the hour seems darkest that is when you need to be optimistic.'

'Optimistic,' said Omelette. 'Right. Fine.'

'Very well. But remember this. At the first sign of a grumble or a sulk from you, I shall walk away and leave you.'

'I won't grumble. Honestly.' He crossed his heart enthusiastically.

'Well, we'll see,' said Eric. He looked up at the trees. 'Now what we must do is walk so that we don't go in a circle.' He began to mumble to himself and walk up and down. Omelette kept silent for he knew that Eric was thinking.

'Notice the trees?' he said suddenly. 'Nearly all of them lean the same way.'

Omelette looked up. It was true. All the trees did lean one way.

'If we always walk so the trees lean away from us we're bound to come out of this forest some time.'

Omelette looked at Eric in amazement. He remembered the promise he had made about always being cheerful and optimistic. He would try it. A huge grin split his face.

'Oh, I should think so, Eric. We'll be out in no time. Nothing to it.'

'Come on then,' said Eric.

Once more the two lost creatures began to trek through the darkness of the forest. They walked for hours, always following the leaning pattern of the trees. Omelette was really feeling very tired but he remembered his promise. Every now and then he would catch up with Eric in order to demonstrate how cheerful he was being.

'I think we're doing awfully well. This must be the right way,' he would chirp cheerily. Or, 'I'm feeling very cheerful being lost in this dark, dangerous forest, aren't you, Eric?' Or, 'I'm sure we'll be out and home soon. I'm in a tremendously optimistic frame of mind.'

After three hours of this Eric stopped and looked at him.

'It's possible to overdo the cheerfulness, you know,' he said.

Omelette looked crestfallen. 'I was only doing what you told me.'

'I understand,' said Eric, 'but can we just walk in silence?'

'Silence?'

'For a bit.'

Omelette nodded. For an hour he followed Eric in silence. Whenever Eric looked at him he smiled and nodded. But despite his cheerful exterior he was feeling quite miserable. They seemed to have been walking for hours. He wondered if there was an end to the forest. Perhaps it went on for ever and ever.

Then suddenly Eric stopped in his tracks. 'Listen!' he said.

Omelette cocked his head. He heard a distant roaring. What could it be? They advanced a few paces. There it was again, only louder. Was it a wild creature of the wood? A monster? Omelette began to back away but Eric pulled him forward.

'We must go on.'

'Must we?' said Omelette, without conviction.

'The alternative is to return to the forest. We must face this new danger together. Are you with me?'

Omelette looked behind him. Suddenly the forest didn't seem such a bad place.

'I'm with you,' he said. Try as he might he couldn't keep the quaver out of his voice.

'Come on then. Let's keep together.'

That was an unnecessary piece of advice. The two friends advanced towards the enemy side by side. And the closer they got the louder the awful roaring sounded.

Seven

With a beating heart Omelette followed Eric through the trees towards the source of the noise. Once the goat turned and shouted something over his shoulder but the roar of the monster carried his words away. The trees were thinner now; they were clearly approaching the forest edge. Then as Omelette rounded a large rock he found himself enveloped in a thin damp mist and Eric seemed to disappear.

He stumbled forward. 'Eric! Eric!' he shouted. But he couldn't hear his own voice. What could he do against so mighty a monster whose roaring could fill the skies and whose breath was an all-enveloping fog? And then a figure emerged out of the mist. It was Eric, shouting and waving to him. Omelette ran towards him and found himself on a high cliff.

'There's your monster,' said Eric, pointing.

Omelette followed his gaze. Beneath them a huge cataract of silver and white water unloaded itself in a great arc into the foaming river hundreds of feet below.

'Waterfall!' shouted Eric in his ear.

'What?'

'WATERFALL!'

For a few minutes they gazed, mesmerised at the falling column of water. Then they galloped along the cliff edge. After a while Omelette began to feel tired.

'What are you doing?' Eric asked, frowning.

'Resting,' said Omelette rather crossly. He'd walked a long way that day. He thought he deserved a rest.

'Why?'

'I'm tired that's why,' said Omelette morosely.

'I'm tired too, but I'm not stopping to rest.'

'It's all right for you, you've got four legs, I've only got two.'

Eric frowned. 'You're sulking again. You know what I warned you about sulking. Isn't that a fowl all over! At the least sign of hardship they give up.'

Omelette hated being called a fowl. His feathers bristled.

'Don't you call me a fowl.'

'Well, don't sulk then. If there's one thing I can't stand it's creatures who whinge and sulk and complain.'

'I didn't ask you to like me,' said Omelette petulantly. To tell the truth he didn't like sulking either, but somehow he couldn't help himself. And once he'd started it was difficult to stop.

'Who said I liked you?' snorted Eric. 'Who could possibly like a stupid fowl who's covered in feathers and sulks and moans all the time?'

Omelette stood up. 'Well, at least I don't have stupid whiskers and walk around on high heels.'

Eric's eyes blazed. 'They're not high heels. For your information they're called hooves.'

'High heels.'

'Well, I'd rather have hooves and whiskers than a pair of wings that can't even help you to fly. I never saw anything so silly in all my life.'

They stared angrily at one another.

'Now are you coming or not?' said Eric.

46

'No,' said Omelette. He sat down and deliberately looked away.

'Well, it's your look out,' said Eric. 'I can't wait for you. If you want to stay here, on your head be it.'

'On your head be it,' repeated Omelette mockingly, waggling his head from side to side. Eric snorted angrily, turned on his heel and began striding away. Omelette watched him. How ridiculous he looked, he thought to himself, swaying from side to side on his silly hooves with his scrag of a tail hanging limply behind him, trying to look dignified.

'You know what you look like? You look stupid,' he shouted after him. 'Stupid, stupid, stupid!' But Eric continued to march away ignoring the taunts.

Eric was almost out of earshot. Omelette screamed, 'I never want to see you again, you stupid goat!'

But if he heard, Eric gave no sign of it.

'D'you hear?' screamed Omelette.

Eric got smaller and smaller. Omellete watched him. A wave of sadness swept over him replacing the anger. 'Eric,' he whispered, 'Eric, don't go. Please come back.'

'ERIC!' he called at the top of his voice. 'ERIC!'

But Eric was out of earshot.

Omelette walked sadly to the edge of the cliff and gazed down at the rolling, foam-flecked river. He wondered if somewhere along its length was the farm. Perhaps if he walked along the riverside he would eventually reach it. But which way? Eric would know. But Eric was no longer with him. A shadow fell across him and from somewhere came a rush of wind. For a second he thought a storm was brewing. The next moment, he felt himself struck as though by a rock and he was bowling across the ground towards the edge of the cliff. He scrabbled with his claws for a foothold but then he was over and falling. He saw the sky tilt and turn. Then the river. He tried to dig his claws into the rockface but he was falling too quickly and then, suddenly, he wasn't falling any more. A thin tree had broken his fall. He lay cradled in the fork of two branches. The tree swayed and creaked. The branch he was on began to creak and bend. Hundreds of feet beneath him the river tumbled, a mass of white water. Gingerly he edged himself back towards the narrow ledge leading up to the top of the cliff, and out of which the sapling grew. As his feet hit the ledge he breathed a sigh of relief. He looked up. He thought he had been falling for hours but in fact it had only been about ten feet. He managed to half crawl, half fly upwards to the top of the cliff. It was then that he saw the enemy waiting for him.

Two cruel but brilliant yellow eyes pierced him. It had a huge open beak, wickedly curved, and wings spread on either side of his body like huge sails. It was the first time that Omelette had seen a golden eagle. He had never before seen a creature so consumed with violence and anger. He was almost paralysed with terror. He uttered a feeble cry and attempted to make his escape, scuttling for the protection of some rocks to his right. The eagle gathered himself and swooped across the plateau, his great wings beating the air, his curved talons out-thrust like hooked knives.

For Omelette it was as though a mountain had fallen on him. One great claw raked his side and he felt himself rolling over and over and over before striking a large boulder. He shook himself. The blow made his head spin.

And then the eagle came in for the kill. Abject with pain and terror, his spirits faint and dizzy, the little bantam crushed himself as far as he could beneath the shelter of

the boulder. The curved beak struck with terrible ferocity across the stone. In his fury the eagle began to tear at the ground. Again and again the cruel talons flashed out. Omelette closed his eyes and cowered as deep as he could into the shelter of the rock. He heard a dull thud. But nothing happened. Fearfully he opened one eye. What he saw made him cry aloud in wonder. The eagle no longer faced him. He had another opponent. An opponent who stood, his four legs spread in defiance, his eyes glaring proud and fearless at the eagle.

'Eric!' Omelette shouted. 'You came back.'

'Think I'd desert a friend in danger? Not my style, old chap.'

He was speaking to Omelette but his eyes never left the eagle. The wings were wide spread now and the neck arched forward as the great bird gathered himself.

'Watch out for his claws!' shouted Omelette.

'Don't you worry,' called Eric.

He had hardly finished speaking when the eagle was upon him. There was a whirlwind of wings and hooves and claws. It was difficult to separate the two. The noise that rose from their throats was terrible. One moment the eagle was above Eric, his beak slashing at his throat. The next they were scuttling across the earth sending the dust and pebbles flying. Then the eagle flew crazily into the air, flung there by Eric's horns. But soon he was back again, his claws striking at Eric's head. A blow from his wings sent Eric crashing against the boulder. For a moment he lay there completely stunned. The eagle advanced, his beak flailing at the goat's unprotected belly.

'Eric!' screamed Omelette in terror. He darted from the rock and sunk his beak with all the strength he could muster into the eagle's neck and hung on. With a shake of his head the eagle sent him crashing into the boulder. To Omelette's amazement Eric cowered away from the eagle. 'Please, no more,' he whimpered, 'I've had enough.'

Omelette couldn't believe that it was Eric who was saying these things. The eagle drew himself up and approached in triumph ready to deliver the final blow. Eric bowed his head in fear. Then suddenly the goat uncoiled himself into a huge jarring kick. The blow exploded against the eagle's breast, sending him careering sideways. Eric turned ready for the next assault. But there was no need. The eagle climbed to his feet and for a moment, on that high plateau beneath the scorching sun, the three creatures faced each other. Then the eagle spread his wings and almost noiselessly lifted into the air and arched away over the gorge. Very soon he was a speck in the blue and then he was gone. For ever.

The two friends looked at one another in amazement and triumph. They both felt they should say something but couldn't decide what. Omelette felt a strange sensation in his throat. He wasn't sure what it was. It was a feeling he'd never had before. Joy and laughter and pride and sadness all mixed together. He opened his beak but what emerged was a rather pathetic giggle. Once started it wouldn't cease. Eric followed suit. The giggle became a titter, the titter a chuckle, the chuckle a laugh and the laugh became an uncontrollable, unstoppable hysterical guffaw. They began to dance on the spot and then round and round one another, their laughter rising to the heavens. They didn't stop until they were too exhausted to dance or laugh any more and flopped on to their backs on the ground and gazed at the sky.

'We saw him off, didn't we?' shouted Eric.

'We? It was you, Eric. The way you kicked him.'

Eric thought about it. He couldn't help smiling. 'Yes, I suppose I did, didn't I,' he said, pride mixed with modesty.

'I thought he'd beaten you. You surrendered.'

'That was called being wily,' said Eric.

'Wily?'

'Something my father taught me. Surprise is the best tactic.'

'It surprised the eagle, all right. Taught him a lesson.'

Eric turned to him. 'But I couldn't have done it without you, old friend. I was nearly done for there for a moment.'

Omelette was secretly proud of the part he had played in the battle but he thought it not proper to admit it.

He shrugged his shoulders and scuffed at the ground in embarrassment. 'Oh that,' he said, blushing slightly, 'that was nothing. Anybody would do the same for a friend.'

51

The mention of the word 'friend' reminded them both of the argument they had had earlier. They looked at one another and both knew that the fight with the eagle somehow had sealed their friendship for ever.

Something caught Omelette's eye. An eagle's feather. He picked it up and stuck it behind Eric's ear.

'Spoils of war,' said Eric. He stared across the valley. 'We ought to celebrate our victory,' he said.

Omelette looked at him. 'What should we do?'

'Well, I could stand to attention and stare into the distance rather nobly and you, well, you could give us a bit of a song, you see. That's the way to do it.'

'But there's nobody about.'

'*We're* about, old thing. We're about.'

'Of course,' said Omelette. 'And anyway that eagle might hear us.'

'Yes, rub it in a bit.'

'Teach him not to try it again.'

And so while Eric drew himself up nobly, his eyes on the blue and distant, Omelette raised up his voice and crowed as loudly as he was able. His best friend would not have called his voice beautiful but it was distinctive and carried effectively. So when Eric said, 'Nobody sings quite like you, my friend,' they both knew what he meant and that he was trying to be kind.

When the song had ended they walked on along the edge of the cliff in silence. Omelette longed to know where they were going but Eric's brow was wrinkled and he kept making little grunting noises to himself. Omelette knew from past experience that this meant he was thinking. Eric didn't like to be interrupted when he was thinking, so he remained silent. After a time though he could stand it no longer.

'Eric,' he began.

'Mmh?' said Eric.

'Do we know where we are going?'

'Yes,' said Eric and after a pause, 'and no.'

'I see,' said Omelette. He looked across the river. There were fields on the other side and trees.

'Couldn't we cross to the other side?'

'It's always greener on the other side,' said Eric.

Omelette looked. 'It looks the same colour to me.'

'It's a saying,' said Eric. 'It means people are never satisfied.'

'I see,' said Omelette. He wondered if Eric thought he was complaining so he stopped talking for a time. Then he got bored with not talking and ran on ahead because he could never wait to see what was round the next corner. What he found there made him call excitedly to Eric.

Eight

Eric found Omelette standing beside a rope bridge. It swayed gently in the wind. Eric plucked at the rope. It was rotted to a single strand. Far beneath their feet the river wound its way across the floor of the canyon.

A flash of lightning split the sky and the thunder rumbled distantly. As the first drops of rain began to fall, Omelette pushed the rope. The bridge swung crazily from side to side. A broken piece of wood dropped slowly into the river.

'It would never hold our weight,' said Eric.

'Ssh!' hissed Omelette. 'Listen.'

'What is it?'

'Someone there!'

'Where?'

'The other side. Listen.'

Omelette threw back his head and sang once more. He paused.

There was a silence and then, distantly from the other side of the valley, came an answering cry.

'Do you hear?' said Omelette excitedly.

'What about it?' said Eric.

'Can't you hear? That song, it came from the other side.'

'But . . .' began Eric.

'Sssh.'

Omelette crowed once more. They both listened. Across the gorge, distantly the cry was answered.

'There, you hear that? Where there's crowing there must be a farm. And where there's a farm there must be food and warmth and shelter.'

'But . . .'

Omelette was too excited to listen.

'I'm going to find out.'

'Don't be stupid,' shouted Eric.

'I'm going to find them,' shouted Omelette. He ran at the bridge and leapt on to it.

Eric shouted a warning but Omelette was in no mood to listen. The rain began to fall in sheets making the rickety bridge slippery and treacherous. It swung beneath him. He clung on for dear life. 'Don't look down,' he repeated to himself under his breath. 'Don't look down. Might be better not to look at all.'

He closed his eyes tight shut and with little steps he began to run for the opposite side. 'Must be nearly there now,' he thought to himself. The bridge began to rise, slowing his advance. Against his better judgement he stopped and opened his eyes. Far beneath him he saw the yellow torrent roaring, dashing itself in angry froth against huge boulders. The lightning flashed once more and the thunder cracked. Omelette's eyes stung with the rain; he could hardly see. He peered through the murk. Almost there. He drew another deep breath and scuttled as fast as his legs would carry him across the remaining few yards and flung himself gratefully on to the safety of the grass. For a few seconds he lay there saying 'Thank you, thank you,' to nobody in particular. Then he rose to his feet and waved triumphantly.

'Nothing to it,' he called.

Eric waved back.

Omelette lifted his voice. What he wanted to say was 'Whooopeee,' but what came out was his normal rather rough and ready morning call, though perhaps with more relief in it than was normal. To his amazement he heard the answering call ringing back to him. He was puzzled. The other cockerel seemed now to be on the bank he had just left. He couldn't understand it.

'Eric,' he called.

'*Eric,*' the voice sang back.

'Hello,' shouted Eric.

'My brothers seemed to have crossed to the other side.'

'*Side, side, side,*' repeated a voice.

'I told you,' shouted Eric, 'but you wouldn't listen. There never was a farm; it was just an echo.'

'Echo,' called Omelette.

'*Cho, cho, cho,*' his own voice came back to him.

'You mean there was nobody?'

'*Body,*' sang the echo, '*body, body, body.*'

Omelette threw himself on to the ground in dismay.

'You'd better come back,' called Eric.

Omelette nodded. He rose to his feet, but when he stopped on the bridge he froze.

'I can't do it!' he screamed, utterly terrified.

Eric could see what had happened.

'Hang on!' shouted Eric. 'I'm coming over.'

He leapt on to the rope and began to walk across. The bridge held no fears for him. Mountain goats spent their lives clambering along narrow ledges or descending steep and hazardous mountain paths. Halfway across he even performed a little dance. Omelette waved to him. And then suddenly a bolt of lightning exploded close to where Omelette was standing. Smoke came from the ground and there was the smell of wood burning. The ash tree to which the rope bridge was attached had split from top to bottom. It leaned dangerously towards the chasm and its roots began to show. A strand of the rope snapped. The bridge lurched.

'Hurry,' screamed Omelette, 'the bridge is falling!'

'*Ing, ing, ing,*' returned the echo.

And then with an awful tearing sound the tree was wrenched from the ground. For a split second Omelette saw the fear in Eric's eyes. It was as though time had stopped. For a second the bridge seemed to hang unsupported in space. Everything stood still. And then, with a terrible suddenness the bridge was gone, plunging into the emptiness beneath. Omelette saw Eric's body falling, falling white and free, looking idiotically small in the vastness of the canyon. Over and over he tumbled before crashing into the black waters of the river. The tattered bridge careered into the cliff face and hung there swaying uselessly.

'Eric!' Omelette screamed.

He peered over the cliff into the murkiness of the river far beneath him. But only the dark waters tossed and tumbled. Of Eric there was no sign.

Frozen with horror and disbelief Omelette gazed down at the water, seeing nothing but turbulent waves. But then Eric appeared, suddenly thrown up like a cork out of the depth of the water.

'Eric!' he screamed, but his voice was carried by the roar of the torrent and the rolling thunder. Eric looked so frail against that black mass of tumbling water. Now and then the river seemed to swallow him down only to spit him out again further downstream where he would bob crazily amongst the careering jetsom of broken trees and empty oil drums.

Shouting aloud Omelette raced, stumbling along the cliff top, trying to keep his friend in sight. The path dropped suddenly towards the river. He slid and ran and scrambled down the uneven slope careless of his own safety. At last he found himself racing through meadow grass and bog land. The brambles clutched at him and the mud sucked him down. But he kept on. Now and then he would glimpse the glint of river water through the trees. It was broader here and more flat. He stopped and gazed anxiously upstream. A pale glint caught his eye. It drifted towards him.

'Eric!' he screamed. 'Eric!'

He ran to the bank only to see a large, white plastic bag swollen by the water floating towards him.

Eric must already have passed. He raced on down the stream, one eye on the water. For more than a mile he ran. But of Eric there was no sign. Perhaps he had been thrown ashore further upstream. Gloomily he retraced his steps. The rain had stopped now and a pale sun slid out from behind a bank of clouds. He whimpered softly to himself.

He came upon a place where the river turned in a violent circle; a whirlpool. A packing case floated downstream. The turning water dragged it slowly into its centre until it disappeared from sight, sucked down by that hungry mouth. No living thing could survive its force.

Something small and brown caught his eye, floating in the shallows at the river's edge. He picked it up gently and held it up to the sun. It was a feather. An eagle's feather. He looked dumbly from the feather to the whirlpool and then back again. Somewhere in the depths of his being where there was no room for lies he felt with an awfulness almost too terrible to bear that his friend had been drowned. He stood there and sobbed; staring for a long time at the spot where he had last seen Eric.

After a time he lay down in the shelter of a willow tree on the bank of the river. He didn't really care what happened to him. He would lie there close to the place where his old friend had been snatched from him; he would lie there until he was dead himself. Darkness fell and the moon shone on the face of the river. And he fell into that deep sleep where no dreams come.

But in a deep cave beyond the river's reach, Eric lay unconcious but alive, and knew none of these things.

When Omelette awoke the afternoon sun burned hot on his feathers. He looked about him and saw the eagle's feather beached in the shingle. The awful memories swept over him and tears came again. What must he do? He must remember this place always, that was important; fix it in his memory for ever so that when he looked back into his memory it would be there always. That willow tree, the grass at the edge of the river, the dark wood at his back.

He began to scratch at the gravel and pebbles. For an hour he dug and soon a small mound took shape at the water's edge. When it was finished he stood back and inspected what he had made. It was good work. If he came back, he would know this place. Something more was needed. He picked up the eagle feather and stuck it firmly into the top of the stone pile. It fluttered bravely in the breeze.

'Goodbye, old friend,' he whispered.

Then he turned his back for ever on that place and continued his way downstream. Where he was going he did not know, but somewhere in the back of his mind the word 'home' called to him. And behind him the river washed against the shore and did not know what it had done.

Nine

All that long afternoon Omelette followed the river. The sun beat down and his stomach grumbled. He realised he had eaten nothing for two days. He found himself in a disused barn with a broken waterwheel. There he rested for an hour managing to find a few specks of corn. But they were old and did little to cure his hunger.

As he left the barn his heart quickened when he saw something on the floor. It was a feather. He inspected it closely. It was just like his. His heart lifted at the thought of company. Then he noticed another feather. And another. With a sudden disappointment he realised they were his *own* feathers. He inspected his right shoulder. There, to the right of his neck was a white patch of flesh. He tugged at one or two feathers. They came out without any difficulty. He realised he was moulting. Perhaps it was to do with the shock of Eric's death. He had heard of such things. He found himself thinking about his friend once more and how he missed him. Quite naturally he began to talk to him out loud.

'What shall I do? Where shall I go?' he asked.

He seemed to hear Eric's voice sounding in his head. 'Keep on,' it said.

'But where to? I'm tired and hungry and unhappy.'

'Never mind,' the voice said, 'something will turn up. It always does.'

And the voice was right. Round the next corner something indeed did turn up. In fact what turned were Omelette's feet as he missed his footing on a patch of mud and slid down a steep, slippery bank. He flapped his wings and tried to grip the ground with his claws but it was no use. He slithered and tumbled and bounced head over heels and the last thing he remembered was his head striking something hard.

About ten minutes later, when he came to, there was an awful aching in his head and a roaring in his ears. He shook his head but the roaring would not go away. He seemed to be rocking from side to side. He looked about him. With a gasp he realised he was not alone. He found himself looking into a cruel mouth full of sharp teeth. Above the teeth two watery eyes stared at him blankly. The whole world seemed to be swaying. Where could he be? Was he dreaming? Then the teeth were no longer there and he was sliding and rolling on something wet and slippery. Trees moved past, and beneath him water flashed. He was on a small motor boat. That explained the swaying sensation and the roaring in his ears. The boat tipped suddenly and he was sent sliding back where he came from. Once more he found himself staring into that vacant watery eye and the sharp teeth. He realised he was lying under a canvas with three dead salmon. To his right were two brace of pheasants. They dangled lifeless from a hook and their eyes stared sightlessly at him. Omelette shuddered. How easily *he* could have been one of them.

'Them pheasants do a treat for supper,' he heard a rough voice exclaim.

Very carefully he raised a corner of the canvas and squinted out. He saw two huge boots and a thick pair of legs clad in dirty mole-skin trousers. At the rear of the boat a taller man was steering. He was unshaven and his teeth were black and broken. He drank from a whisky bottle. On his left cheek just beneath his eye was a tattoo of two crossed swords and beneath it a long red scar. To his horror Omelette realised he was sharing the boat with the two men who had rustled the Westmorelands' farm two nights earlier. Not daring to breathe he lowered the canvas and lay still. But he couldn't keep his beak from chattering.

'Here,' the man called Harry said, pointing at the scar, 'I'd like to meet the rooster what give me this. Know what I'd do?' He twisted an imaginary neck in his big hands and made the sound of a neck being broken. The other man laughed and Omelette shivered with fear.

'Here, Snouty boy, get us another bottle.'

'Get it yourself.'

'I can't get it. I'm steering.'

'Where is it?'

'Underneath that canvas somewhere.'

Omelette froze. He looked for somewhere to hide but there was nowhere to go. He cowered beneath the canvas making himself as small as possible. He felt the boat sway as the man leaned forward; saw his huge hand feeling blindly under the canvas. He cowered, but the hand seemed to crawl after him like a huge spider.

'Get a move on, Snouty, ain'tcha found it yet? I'm dying of first 'ere.'

Omelette pushed the bottle towards the groping hand. It closed on it. 'Bingo!' yelled Snout. 'One bottle of whisky comin' up.'

Omelette breathed a sigh of relief. He heard the bottle being opened and the sound of drinking. Then the man called Snout said:

'Here, Harry, we better not let the Old Man see us

63

bringing this lot in.'

'What can he do?'

'He'll murder us, Harry. You know he don't like us hunting fish and birds out of season, Harry.'

'How's he gonna know about it? Gone to market, ain't he?'

'We should have been working in the barn.'

Harry swore angrily. 'Work, work, work. That's all we do. And for what? For nothing.'

'That's right, Harry. For nothing. I mean it's Saturday. We should be out having a good time like everybody else.'

'We are out having a good time, Snouty, so what's the difference.' And Harry laughed once more. 'Anyway, what if he does catch us? I ain't scared of him like you.'

Snout laughed weakly. 'I ain't scared of him.'

'Don't give me that. You, you're scared of your own shadow.'

Omelette wondered how he could escape. He knew there must come a time when the boat would have to be unloaded. They would be sure to find him. He would just have to make a run for it. The sun was going down so at least it would be almost dark. That would give him a better chance. He settled down beneath the canvas to wait.

Eventually he felt a soft bump as the boat came alongside and Harry jumped ashore. A hand reached under the canvas and pulled out the fish. They were linked together by a long line through their gills.

'Sling 'em 'ere. I'll take those,' he heard Harry say. 'You bring the pheasants.'

Snout's hand grasped the canvas. Omelette cowered. There was no escape. Then he had an idea. He bit on to the hook that held the four pheasants with his beak and clung there for dear life trying to look as dead as possible.

'Got 'em?'

'Yeah.'

He felt Snout pick up the hook. The four dead pheasants jostled against him. Would Snout notice that there were now five birds?

Then he heard a strong, deep voice he hadn't heard before.

'What d'you think you've been up to behind my back?'

Omelette opened one eye. He saw an older man with a white beard and glaring eyes. He stood, broad and tall on the bank, his legs spread, his hands on his hips.

'Nothing, Dad, honest,' said Harry nervously.

'Honest?' roared the Old Man. 'Honest! You wouldn't know the meaning of the word. What's that you got there?'

'Nothing, Dad,' said Harry.

'Nothing! Salmon. You pass them here.'

Harry passed the salmon to the Old Man.

'And what's that you've got, mister?'

Snout hid the pheasants and Omelette behind his back.

'Nothing, Dad.'

'Nothing!' the Old Man roared.

Omelette's feet were nearly touching the ground.

'Don't lie to me, boy.'

As carefully as he could Omelette slipped from the hook and dropped to the ground. He crouched behind Snout's legs.

'I'm not lying, Dad,' said Snout.

Omelette could feel his legs trembling with fear.

'Give them to me, mister,' shouted the Old Man, snatching the pheasants.

'Nothing, eh? You don't lie, eh?'

Snout tried to look surprised. 'Just look at that. Pheasants. I wonder how they got there?'

'You killed them, that's how,' said the Old Man, shaking Snout until his teeth rattled. 'I warned you about killing pheasants and salmon out of season.'

'We just found 'em, Dad, honest.'

'Found them? Where?'

Snout stuttered, 'Er . . . er . . .'

'Yeah, that's right, Dad,' said Harry, joining in. 'We was working by the river and we saw these poachers so naturally we went to stop 'em, didn't we, Snout?'

Snout nodded with relief. 'Oh yeah, I remember now. Yeah, we stopped 'em, Dad. What a fight we had, Dad. We took the pheasants off 'em.'

'And the salmon.'

'Yeah, and the salmon.'

While this argument was going on Omelette was creeping backwards, one slow step at a time.

The Old Man roared, 'And where are they?'

'Where's what, Dad?'

'Where are these poachers you so bravely arrested?'

'Ah yes . . . well . . . er . . .'

'They got away, Dad,' said Harry.

'Got away?'

'Yeah, we tried to hold 'em but there was three of 'em.'

'Four,' said Harry.

'Yeah, that's right, four,' agreed Snout, nodding vigorously.

'Well,' said the Old Man, 'I think you deserve to be rewarded for being so brave.' He began to unbuckle his belt. 'You should have something for what you've done. And what I'll give you is a taste of my belt.'

'Oh no, Dad. What for?'

'Because you're liars both of you. There were no poachers. You caught these birds and fish yourself. And you've been drinking again. I can smell the filthy stuff on your breath. What would your mother say. She'll be turning in her grave. You're a disgrace to the family name. You won't go off this farm for the next four weeks. And there'll be extra work from five o'clock every morning. I'll teach you to creep off when you should be working. I'll teach you to lie to me!'

And the Old Man began to kick his two sons towards the farmhouse.

'Ouch!' squealed Harry.

'Ouch!' yelled Snout.

Their voices disappeared into the distance. Omelette raced through the gloom up a steep hill, putting as much distance between himself and the evil brothers as he could. At the top of the hill was a prickly hedge. He scuttled beneath it and found himself in a large field. To the left was the largest, tallest dung heap he had ever seen. At the very top, motionless, upright and proud, silhouetted against the crimson of the evening sky was a magnificent cockerel. Relief flooded over Omelette. He was with friends. He began to run in the direction of the rooster but found himself surrounded by a row of staring hostile eyes.

'And where do you think you're going in such a hurry?' said a threatening voice.

Ten

'You heard what I said. Speak up! Where do you think you're going?'

Omelette found himself looking at two extremely haughty hens. Six or seven others hovered in a circle behind them. Further off more hens gazed at him curiously from the rusty hulks of abandoned cars. There was no hope of escape and even if there had been he was too weak to attempt it.

The two hens inspected him carefully from head to foot.

'Well?'

Omelette's head was spinning. He felt weak from lack of food and his injured wing and bruised foot were aching. He didn't seem to be able to see the two hens clearly. Sometimes there were two and sometimes four. He blinked his eyes. He felt too tired and breathless after his long climb to say anything. He shook his head feebly.

'It doesn't know, Mercedes.'

'Apparently not, Sunbeam. I wonder where it's come from.'

'Well? Answer,' snapped Sunbeam.

'Answer!' chorused the hens. Omelette pointed his wing in the direction of the river.

'Hhm,' sniffed Sunbeam. 'It doesn't know.'

'It's very ugly.'

Sunbeam sniffed. 'And it pongs of fish.'

Omelette hadn't the energy to speak. Mercedes walked up to him and rapped quite hard on the top of his head. 'Hello,' she called. 'Hello, is there anybody in there?'

Omelette felt his anger rising. Didn't they realise they were talking to somebody who had escaped from rustlers, found his way through an unmapped forest, crossed a ravine, fought with an eagle and lived to tell the tale? Hens held no terror for him. He'd show them.

'Charge!' he tried to shout, but his voice was a feeble croak. He advanced towards them but after a couple of yards fell in a heap on the ground. He would have liked to have got up but he felt too tired. Stars swam before his eyes. He decided to stay where he was.

The two hens looked down at him curiously, then they began to talk to one another in whispers. Eventually they nodded their heads and a small bantam with a limp and only one wing leaned over him.

'Up you get, old chap,' he said and helped Omelette to his feet. He was marched along through the farmyard surrounded by a procession of curious hens.

Omelette gazed about him. There seemed to be a mist over his eyes.

'Where are you taking me?' he asked of the little lame bantam, who seemed more friendly than the others.

'The well,' he replied.

'What well?'

'The well we throw our enemies down.'

'What happens to them after?'

'What d'you mean "after"? Nothing happens to them after. They die, that's all.'

'Die!' said Omelette in dismay.

'I shouldn't worry about it,' aid the limping bantam cheerfully. 'That's life. Some go down wells and some

70

don't. No use complaining about it. Like my wing and my leg. Was born like that. All the complaining in the world isn't going to put that right.' He glanced at Omelette. 'What happened to your feathers anyway?'

Omelette looked down. There were great patches of white where the feathers had been. 'They just sort of fell off,' he said.

'There you are then. Name's Morris, by the way. Born in a car. Lot of us born in old cars. See that young hen over there? She's called Bedford. That one there's called Rover, she's Ford, she's Riley, she's Austin and so on. What's yours?'

'What's my what?'

'Name?'

'Omelette.'

'Funny name for a car.'

Omelette thought there might not be time to explain about his name.

'Am I really going to die?'

'Oh yes, I should think so,' said Morris.

Mercedes, who was leading the procession, turned round crossly. 'Keep up and no talking.'

Morris whispered. '*She's* number one wife.'

'Who's wife?'

'Why Aragon's of course.'

'Who's Aragon?'

'Who's Aragon?' Morris spluttered in surprise. 'Aragon's our leader. Rooster. Very impressive. You'll like him.'

'Like him! But he's going to throw me down the well.'

'Well, there is that, I suppose. But then nobody's perfect.'

Omelette contemplated the swaying tail feathers of

71

Mercedes and Sunbeam who were revelling in the attention the arrest of a stranger had given them. He thought about Eric and his safe home at the Westmorelands' farm that he would never see again. His shoulders began to shake. Tears started from his eyes. 'I don't want to die,' he sobbed.

'That's natural, I suppose. But what can I do?'

Omelette thought about this. 'Couldn't you look the other way while I escape?'

'Look the other way? Let you escape? And what do you suppose happens to me? They'd throw me down instead. Look at it from my point of view.'

Omelette hung his head. This time there seemed no escape.

Morris glanced up at the bantam.

'Can I give you a bit of advice?'

'Yes.'

'Try to die nobly.'

'Nobly?'

'Yes. Head up, proud, defiant. That sort of thing. It'll please Aragon. Likes that sort of thing, you see. If you die crying and squealing you'll upset him no end.'

'Well, I don't want to upset anyone while I'm dying,' Omelette responded rather bitterly.

Morris stopped him and looked into his eyes. 'Look,' he said confidentially, 'I've taken a shine to you. Maybe it's because of your limp and your moulting. You even make me look reasonable. I can't promise anything but if there's something I *can* do, I will.'

'But what?'

'Ssh, we're here. I've said enough already.'

The procession had arrived at an open yard on one side of which was a large stone farmhouse. At the other end

72

was a well with a handle and a large bucket attached to a rope. Three of the hens raised Omelette on to a wooden barrel beside the well. He was too weak to stand and tried to sit down but each time that he did they raised him up again. His eyes kept wanting to close.

The hens all looked at him. Suddenly there was the sound of cheering and the hens parted. Through the cheering avenue they formed strode the cockerel Omelette had seen earlier. His feathers were of a shimmering gold, flecked with blue and iridescent green. His eyes glittered with a fierce pride and his fine head was crowned with a magnificent scarlet crop that bounced as he walked. He turned and faced the multitude raising one wing imperiously.

'It is we,' he declared loftily and the hens cheered even louder.

'Ar-a-gon, Ar-a-gon,' they chanted.

'Quite right,' said Aragon smiling. He raised his wing and there was an immediate silence.

He brushed some imaginary dirt off the green feathers that covered most of his legs. 'And who is the greatest in the land?' he murmured.

'Aragon, Aragon,' sang the hens in unison.

'Got it in one,' murmured Aragon softly. 'And don't you forget it.'

He peered at Omelette. 'Not very big, are we. Not very pretty either. You realise the penalty for intruding on my domain, I suppose.'

Omelette shook his head.

Aragon walked round him. 'There can only be one cockerel, only one leader here and naturally that's we. Of course there's Morris but he doesn't count. He's a runt. What are you, Morris?'

73

'A runt, Your Magnificence.'

'Quite. You, on the other hand, although bald, although extraordinarily ugly are not a runt and therefore and therefore . . .'

Aragon sniffed. 'What's that appalling pong?' he asked putting his wing to his beak.

'It's fish, Your Eminence.'

'Fish?'

'The accused here smells of fish.'

Aragon looked down his beak at Omelette and moved a few paces down wind.

'Oh well, that settles it. Down the well with him.'

The multitude cheered.

'But I'm innocent,' said Omelette.

'Well, you would say that, wouldn't you?' murmured Aragon. 'To the well with the culprit.'

Cheering, the hens dragged poor Omelette protesting to the edge of the well. Omelette felt himself being forced towards the rim. A heavy rock was tied about his neck and he was stretched out face-down on the parapet. He looked down and saw the well disappearing into darkness. It appeared to have no end. He dislodged a small pebble. He didn't hear it splash. Perhaps the well had no bottom. Panic rose in him.

'One!' shouted the hens and began to swing Omelette back and forth. In desperation Omelette turned to Morris. 'I thought you were going to help me.'

'I *am* trying to help you,' said Morris.

'Think of something,' hissed Omelette urgently.

'I'm trying to think of something.'

'Two!' shouted the hens.

'Have you thought of something?' said Omelette.

The hens drew a deep breath. Omelette was rocked

74

back for the third and last time. They were just about to
say 'Three' when someone shouted 'Stop' in such a
commanding voice that they all stood still.

Aragon looked about him. 'Who said that?'

'I did, Eminence,' said Morris.

'What is it? If you're just wasting my time again you'll
be down the well too.'

'Your Worship,' he said, confidentially sidling up to
Aragon, 'might I have a word?'

'Is it important?'

'I believe so. It was really about how magnificently you
sing.'

'Oh really.' Aragon looked more cheerful at this news.
'Well, carry on then.'

'Yes. I thought of a way you could make it sound even better.'

Aragon looked at Morris peevishly. 'Are you, in some round-about way, trying to tell me that there is room for improvement?'

'Oh no, Your Worship, no, what I was suggesting was how you could *appear* to be even more wonderful.'

'Appear. Ah. How?'

Morris put on a mysterious expression and spoke in a strange voice. 'Does not the sun shine brighter from between dark clouds?'

'Dark clouds? Sunshine? What are you talking about? For heaven's sake stop talking in riddles.'

'Very well,' said Morris. 'It is impossible to make you sound or look more magnificent than you are already. But suppose,' said Morris conspiratorially, tapping the side of his beak, 'suppose you had as a constant companion, somebody stunted and ugly with a voice like a combine harvester with laryngitis, wouldn't your glory appear to shine even more brightly by comparison. Mmh?'

Morris could see that Aragon was captivated by the idea.

'Yes, I see.' He looked out of the corner of his eye at Omelette and nudged Morris. 'You mean the . . . er . . . Bald One here might . . . er . . .'

'Exactly, Your Eminence.'

'You've heard him sing?'

'I'm afraid so.'

'What? Was it pretty bad?'

'Appalling, Your Eminence.'

'We . . . er . . . ought to er . . . hear him.'

Morris bowed. He walked over to Omelette and drew him on one side.

He whispered in Omelette's ear. 'Listen, just do what I tell you. I want you to sing as badly as you can.'

'Sing?'

'Yes.'

'Badly?'

'Atrociously.'

'But everybody will laugh at me.'

Morris seized him. 'What do you think of being thrown down the well?'

'Not much,' said Omelette.

'Exactly. So if you want to save yourself sing as badly as you know how. Understand?'

Omelette nodded. 'I'll try my best.'

'Worst,' said Morris.

Morris patted him on the back and winked. He walked over to Aragon. 'He's ready to sing now, Your Eminence.'

Aragon waved for silence. 'Quiet, everybody.'

The hens looked up with hushed expectancy. Aragon looked at Omelette.

'Sing!' he instructed.

And Omelette opened his beak and sang. At the best of times his voice had not been noted for its quality. Now, what with the dangers he had faced, the hunger and the sickness in his head and stomach, his voice was weaker than ever. He sang as flatly and raucously as he knew how. After the first few notes the hens stared at one another in disbelief. They began to murmur amongst themselves. Finally they put their wings over their ears and began to moan. At last Omelette stopped.

Morris walked over to Aragon. 'Well, Your Eminence?'

'I don't know,' muttered Aragon. 'It was pretty awful but to be frank I was hoping for worse.'

'He could practise,' suggested Morris.

'You think so?'

'Oh, yes.'

'Mmh,' murmured Aragon. 'Very well. We'll give it a try.' He raised his voice. 'Let the prisoner go. There will be no execution today.'

The assembled hens gave a groan of disappointment and departed muttering amongst themselves.

Aragon took Morris on one side, 'Look here, Morris, you look after the Bald One tonight. Find him somewhere to sleep and tell him to report at the dung heap just before sunrise for singing practice and er . . .' Aragon looked round furtively, 'no need to say a word to anyone about our little arrangement. Don't want to appear vain, catch my drift?'

'Quite, Your Eminence.'

'Good fellow,' said Aragon, and stalked off with Sunbeam and Mercedes in tow.

'Does that mean I'm saved?' asked Omelette.

Morris nodded. 'I told you I'd think of something, didn't I? You see, even being ugly can have its advantages.'

Omelette thought about it. Morris was right.

Eleven

The next morning, just before sunrise, Omelette reported to the dung heap for his singing lesson. Aragon was already there. Omelette remembered Morris's advice and tried to look as shabby and ugly as possible.

First of all Aragon made him walk up and down while he watched him from the top of the dung heap.

'Far too spritely,' shouted Aragon. 'Hang your head more and drag the feet.'

Omelette did as he was told. His wings trailed in the dust.

'Good, that's a lot worse,' said Aragon. 'Now then, try walking behind me. Ready? Off we go.'

And as Aragon marched in a circle, upright, majestic and proud, Omelette followed behind trying to look as dishevelled as possible.

Aragon glanced over his shoulder at him. 'Fine,' he shouted. 'Just keep that up.'

Omelette smiled.

'Now it's time for your singing lessons. One – Two – Three – Bad singing, begin.'

And Omelette sang. He tried his very best to make his voice as croaky and tuneless as he could. When his song came to an end he looked up at Aragon who was shaking his head.

'That will never do. You're not even trying. There were even a few notes in tune there. Come on. Worse! Worse!'

So Omelette tried again. Perhaps it was the fear of the well, but a terrible caterwauling unwound into the morning air, and the more Omelette sang the more hideous the sound became.

At last he stopped, and stood there panting for breath. He had never thought that singing badly could be such hard work.

'Splendid,' said Aragon, applauding. He coughed. 'Now it is our turn.'

He climbed to the top of the dung hill and launched into his morning call. From his gaudy throat poured a flood of glorious sound. It rang in Omelette's ears like silver bells. Across the valley it wound its way. There were trills and peaks and hollows. It roared to a great crescendo then fell to an almost inaudible whisper before exploding once again just when you least expected it. Omelette had never heard anything to equal it. From the assembled hens came a thunder of applause. Omelette couldn't help but join in.

Aragon smiled and waved. He was content. His plan was working.

Omelette too was contented. Being Aragon's slave was a small price to pay for the good food he was fed and a warm perch in the hen coop. Always in the back of his mind was the idea that one day he would return home but he needed to recover all his old strength before he could attempt that. After all his adventures he was glad of a quiet life. The hens too treated him with more respect once they saw how Aragon valued him. Each day he grew stronger and his wing hurt less although his feathers still refused to grow. Also, as the days passed, he grew in experience and understanding. He learned for example how much Aragon enjoyed flattery. The more Omelette praised him the happier he seemed to become. Each morning after his aria had finished Omelette would say, 'You certainly are in good voice this morning, maestro.'

Aragon's chest would swell with pride and he would beam and say, 'Do you think so? By Jove, I think you're right. Better than yesterday, you think?'

'Oh, much better, maestro.'

And in this way Aragon came to rely more and more on his little companion.

One morning, towards the end of his second week on the farm as Omelette stood in the grey, before-dawn light studying the horizon, an idea came to him. Normally Aragon waited for the sun to appear before he began his singing but on this particular morning Omelette persuaded him to sing a second or two before dawn broke. As his call echoed into silence, as if by magic, the sun rose over the horizon flooding the hillside in golden light.

'See, maestro,' exclaimed Omelette, 'how the sun rises obedient to your call.'

'By Jove, I believe you're right,' said Aragon and he called the hens to him and pointed at the sun.

'See that!' he shouted gleefully. 'We did that. We sang and bingo! Up it popped.'

And the hens looked up in wonderment.

'A miracle,' they cried. 'Aragon has made another miracle.'

Only Morris knew what was going on. 'The sun would have come up anyway,' he muttered quietly so that no one but Omelette would hear.

'You know that,' said Omelette, 'I know that, but he doesn't know that.'

Morris studied him with a new respect. 'You are turning into what we call a crafty bird,' he said with a wink.

'Well,' explained Omelette, 'if you're not big and strong in this world you have to use your brains.'

As Aragon's standing increased he began to look on Omelette as a kind of lucky charm and would even share his lunch and his secrets with him. During the long afternoons they would scratch out little hollows in the grass and sit contentedly side by side amongst the murmur of bees, watching the world drift lazily by, talking of this and that. Aragon confessed that he had never intended to drop him down the well.

'It's just that it's sort of expected of one. You see, when I get up in front of the crowd it makes me want to do the most awful things. I just can't stop myself.'

'I understand,' said Omelette.

'Do you really? You know, you do cheer me up.' He sighed. 'I say, I'm rather bored. In fact I'm frightfully bored. Come on, Ugly One, tell me a story.'

So Omelette told him of his adventures with the brothers and of the death of Eric. And Aragon listened wide-eyed. He loved stories. Each day he would ask him to tell another story. At first Omelette was worried because he thought he might run out of stories. But he needn't have been concerned. Aragon was quite content to hear the same story over and over again.

And in return Aragon would share his worries with Omelette. One afternoon he told him of his great enemy, Monsieur Ricard, the French fox. 'How he got here nobody knows. Cunning, you see. 'Course my daddy had an up and downer with him. When I was just a chick he came creeping up here one winter, snow on the ground, killed thirteen hens before you could look round. Daddy wasn't afraid. Went for him. Got him by the nose and wouldn't let go. Ricard flung him all over the yard but he just hung on. In the end he made off. Left half his nose behind. Found it next morning by the horse trough. That taught him a lesson, I can tell you. Killed him maybe. I don't know. Haven't seen him for years. But I have a sneaking suspicion he's been around again lately. So if you see a Frenchified fox with only half a hooter, you just yell out "Fox" loud as you can.'

'If he does come around, you'd see him off, wouldn't you, Aragon? Just like your daddy did.'

Aragon looked at him. 'What? Oh yes, yes of course I would.'

There was a silence. The two of them watched the Old Man crossing the farmyard to the barn, a sack of grain on his shoulder. He began to scatter it amongst the hens.

'I say, grub up,' said Aragon, and at the thought of food his despondent mood left him. Together they trotted off towards the farmer.

The weeks went by. The Old Man treated them well. He seemed to know every hen by name and made sure each one had plenty to eat. Sometimes his two sons came out with him and when they did, Omelette made sure he kept out of sight. The Old Man didn't seem to care much for his sons. Everything they said seemed to annoy him and sometimes he would threaten them with his stick. Although they were bigger and younger they seemed to be afraid of him.

One afternoon as Omelette was hiding behind a bale of hay he heard them arguing.

'If you had four batteries you could fit two fousand hens in here, Dad. Batteries. The only way yer going to make money in this game, Dad.'

The old white-haired man turned on them in a fury.

'Batteries!' he shouted. 'Batteries! And what about the hens? Did you ever think of them? Like a living death for them. There'll be no batteries on this farm, not while I'm alive. And you can clean out the pigs tonight for just thinking about it.'

'Oh, Dad. It's Saturday. We was going to town dancing and that.'

'You want to dance, you dance around the pig sty. You mention batteries again and I'll have you off this farm for good and all, sons or no sons.' And the Old Man marched away.

Crouching behind a hay bale Omelette heard Harry curse. 'I can't go on like this. It's like being in gaol. If he keeps on at me I won't be responsible for my actions.'

And he lifted an axe above his head and brought it down into the bale inches from Omelette's head.

That night, as all the hens settled down to sleep in the warmth of the hen coop, Omelette asked Morris if he knew what a battery was.

'Battery!' he said. 'That's a prison camp for hens. A hell on earth. You're all crowded into little wooden cells, one on top of another with hardly enough room to breathe. I've seen hens go mad in there; kill each other in their madness and tear their own feathers out. It's a living death.'

'But they wouldn't do that to us, would they?' asked Omelette.

'Wouldn't they just,' said Morris. 'Snout and Harry would do anything for money. But we're safe as long as the Old Man is alive. He believes in the old ways. But if anything happens to him I wouldn't give much for our chances.'

That night Omelette had a nightmare. He dreamed he was in a battery trying to scratch his way out. Suddenly he awoke. The sound of the scratching continued. He shook himself and wondered if he was still asleep. There was something else. A strong, sharp stench that filled his nostrils. What was it? He'd smelled the same smell that first night in the wood with Eric. Now it was there again and it frightened him now as it had done then.

Scratch, scratch, scratch.

It seemed to be coming from the wooden wall of the hen coop just beneath his perch.

Scratch, scratch, scratch.

He glanced about him fearfully. The other hens were all asleep. He watched fascinated, his eyes fixed on the base of the wall. The earth beneath it seemed to be moving. What could it be? Then a chink of light could be seen. And something else. Like the earth moving but more solid. Then he saw it and he realised what the smell was. He tried to run but his legs were paralysed. He tried to sing out a warning but no sound came. Frozen in horror he watched fascinated as the hole got bigger and bigger. Now half the muzzle of the creature was through and Omelette saw the flashing white of an eye. But that nose . . . there was something strange about it. Half of it seemed to have been eaten away!

And then Omelette found his voice.

Twelve

'FOX!' screamed Omelette at the top of his voice.

'Fox!' cried the hens, suddenly torn from peaceful slumber into waking terror. In a wild panic they flung themselves into the air and hurled their bodies from one side of the shed to the other. Their screams filled the night. Omelette was knocked to the ground by the fluttering bodies. He tried to struggle to his feet but the desperate hens trod him to the ground. And yet there was nowhere to flee. They were trapped. As soon as they reached one wall they turned and rushed hysterically back to where they had come from. A beam in the ceiling cracked and fell to the ground with a crash, bringing part of the roof with it.

'He's coming through the ceiling,' screamed Sunbeam, and the hysteria increased.

Someone hauled Omelette to his feet. It was Morris.

'Are you all right?' he gasped.

'I think so.'

'Where's the fox?' asked Morris.

Omelette pointed. In all the pandemonium the fox continued to dig methodically and calmly, in contrast to the panic within. Already his head was through. His jaws dripped saliva and blood. As his claws scratched at the earth, the hole steadily increased in size. The other hens noticed Omelette and Morris. For an instant there was a strange stillness. They watched in horror as the fox continued with his work. For an instant too the fox stopped his work. Slowly his eyes gazed round the coop. The hens looked back murmuring and shifting but somehow hypnotised by those cruel eyes that seemed to burn through each of them in turn. Omelette felt it too. He tried to tear his eyes away but he could not. That was the way the fox's terror worked. And then as they all gazed at him, transfixed by those unblinking eyes, the fox did a most unexpected thing. His jaws parted and he smiled. He actually smiled. And that smile somehow frightened Omelette more than anything he had ever seen in his life. Then just as suddenly as it had appeared the smile became a snarl and the fox began to dig once more.

Scratch, scratch, scratch.

Now both paws were through. Panic returned like a forest fire that had died for a second and then roared up once more with redoubled force.

'We have to get outside!' shouted Morris.

Omelette could not move. Terror nailed his feet to the floor. He was ashamed of himself but he couldn't help it. His eyes were fixed on the fox and the ever increasing hole.

Scratch, scratch, scratch.

'Come on,' said Morris. 'If we can get outside he might chase us. Leave the rest in peace. We can run towards the oak – once we're in the lower branches, he won't be able to touch us.'

But Omelette was incapable of speech or movement.

Morris disappeared. And still Omelette stared and stared.

Scratch, scratch, scratch.

The sound was like a soft drumbeat in Omelette's brain.

88

Scratch, scratch, scratch.

The fox, bristling and ginger, seemed to be able to dig and gaze about him at the same time. His eye drew Omelette's like a magnet. Then he heard the fox's voice. It whispered in his skull like a nightmare.

'I'm going to get you. You can't get away from Monsieur Ricard. I'm going to get you. I'm going to get YOU!'

Then, out in the night, he heard another voice. At first he couldn't understand. It was Morris's. What was Morris doing outside?

'Come on, Monsieur Ricard,' said the voice. 'What have you got your head in a hole for?'

The fox stopped digging and for a second his eye left Omelette's. For the first time the fox seemed confused.

'Over here, Monsieur Ricard,' sang Morris's mocking

voice. 'I bet you can't catch me. You do look silly with your head in a hole. I think I'll peck you on the bum.'

The fox gave a shriek. His eyes closed in pain and with an angry snarl he hauled his head from the hole.

Outside they could hear Morris laughing uproariously and the fox snarling. Then there was silence. The chickens looked at one another in the settling dust. They were calmer now. The smell of fox was less strong, but it still hung like an infection in the air, hovering in the straw and amongst the rafters.

'Where was Aragon?' they then wondered.

They found him at last, unconscious beneath a piece of wood that had fallen down when the ceiling collapsed. Silently they gathered round him and called his name. Groups of hens gathered together for comfort. Aragon did not move.

'He's dead,' they whispered to one another in horror.

Mercedes laid her head to his chest.

'He's still breathing,' she said.

'Aragon,' cried Sunbeam, 'wake up!'

Aragon sighed gently and his eyes slowly opened. Dazedly he looked round at the hens that crowded about him.

'Where am I?' he groaned. 'What happened?'

The hens all spoke at once.

'There was a fox.'

'He tried to burrow in.'

'It was Monsieur Ricard.'

'A fox,' said Aragon, rising unsteadily to his feet. 'Monsieur Ricard, slayer of my father! Let me at him!'

He made for the door but half a dozen hens clung to him.

'Aragon, don't leave us,' they cried. 'Ricard will kill you.'

'Kill me!' roared Aragon. 'What does death mean to me?'

But still they held him back.

'What should we do if he were to kill you?' they cried. 'We should be all alone.'

Reluctantly Aragon agreed not to venture outside. He ordered them to close up the mouth of the tunnel as best they could. Then they tended to the wounded and comforted the younger and more fearful hens.

Eventually everybody settled down but few slept. There was an uneasy restlessness. Aragon and Omelette agreed to keep guard over the hole in case Monsieur Ricard might decide to return. They marched up and down slowly not saying a word, their senses alert.

Far away on the other side of the valley they heard the triumphant barking of the fox. He was on his way home. He wouldn't be back that night. It was unusual for him not to return without something for his cubs. Omelette thought about Morris alone in the dark, and he feared for his friend. In the barn, an owl shrieked and slowly the dawn came.

Thirteen

In the morning when the Old Man came to feed the hens he discovered the hole.

'Looks like a fox has been here,' he said to himself. He went back to the house and when he returned his two sons were with him carrying guns under their arms.

'You'll both of you stay up tonight in the yard and keep guard,' said the Old Man.

'Dad,' protested Harry, 'we was going out with the lads tonight.'

'You'll be stopping in tonight and every night until this fox is killed.'

'Oh, Dad.'

'Don't you "Oh, Dad" me. Now have a look round, see what you can find.'

The brothers grumbling searched the farm but there was no sign of Monsieur Ricard.

Neither was there any sign of Morris.

Later when the Old Man thought it was safe, the hens were allowed out. They emerged blinking and wary into the sunlight.

That morning Aragon's song was louder and more defiant than usual. He stopped short, though, when Mercedes and Sunbeam came rushing over excitedly.

'Look what we've found,' they said.

Aragon and Omelette followed them to the wire netting

fence that had been tacked to a wooden gate near the farmhouse. The netting had been raised.

'That's where he came through,' said Aragon.

'Look there,' said Omelette.

They inspected the fence more closely. Attached to the wiring was a wisp of ginger hair.

'Monsieur Ricard was here, all right,' said Aragon grimly.

But Omelette wasn't listening. His sharp eyes spotted something on the other side of the fence. Amongst some flattened grass he found a clump of brown feathers: Morris's feathers. And there, staining the grass a dirty red was blood. He called Aragon over. Neither of them could say anything. From the other side of the fence Mercedes called, 'Did you find anything? What is it?'

Aragon looked down at Morris's feathers, and then at Omelette. 'It's nothing,' he called. 'Morris has probably led old Ricard on a wild goose chase. He'll be back soon, mark my words.'

But from the way he spoke Omelette knew that he didn't believe it. He thought about Morris. How he had twice saved his life. Not for the first time he found tears falling from his eyes.

'I know,' said Aragon, trying to comfort him.

'If only I'd gone out with him last night he might still be alive.'

'The best thing we can do for Morris is to try to be as brave as him.'

'Impossible,' said Omelette.

'We'll see. Come on, let's call a meeting.'

They walked slowly in the direction of the farmyard.

'Look here,' Aragon whispered in Omelette's ear, 'don't say anything about this to the others. Cause a panic, d'you see. Morale's low enough as it is. Don't want to make it any worse.'

Omelette nodded.

They walked back towards the hens and Aragon called them all together. He stood on the top of the dung heap and addressed them. For once the hens were still and silent. Not one of them fidgeted. They knew how serious matters were.

'As you all know,' said Aragon, 'our ancient and cunning enemy, Ricard, paid us a call last night. And I have to tell you that he'll be back.'

At these words the hens shifted nervously. One cried out in fear. Aragon continued.

'It may not be tonight. Or the next night or the night after that, but rest assured, he will be back. Now, the Old Man will be more alert.'

'They came round this morning with guns,' shouted out one hen at the back.

Aragon nodded and held up his wings for silence.

'That's correct. But we can't rely on them. You know how heavily they sleep.'

'That's because they're always sozzled,' said Sunbeam.

'Glug, glug,' said another hen and they all laughed.

Aragon's eyes raked the assembly and there was silence once more.

'Now, we know that he crept in under the gate by the farmhouse. So what I propose is that two of us stand guard near the house and if he returns we can raise the alarm. We can't trust the brothers or the dogs. We all know how sly Monsieur Ricard can be. And it doesn't take much cunning to outwit the brothers.'

'Good plan,' murmured the hens approvingly amongst themselves.

94

Omelette wondered who the two would be. He thought about the blood on the grass and the pile of feathers they had found.

'Who will stand guard?' asked Mercedes.

'I, of course, will be one. And the other will be our friend here.'

Omelette looked round to see who Aragon was pointing at. To his dismay he saw that Aragon was pointing directly at him. 'You'll stand by me, won't you?' Aragon said.

All the hens looked at Omelette. There was a long pause. In his head Omelette had a picture of the fox. It was shaking something by the throat. He saw it was himself. His little heart began to pound.

'Well?' demanded Aragon.

Omelette hesitated. Then he thought of Morris, and anger seized him. 'Yes, I'll do it,' said Omelette, trying not to make his voice tremble.

All the hens cheered and those nearest patted him on the back.

'I knew I could rely on you,' said Aragon.

The skies grew dark. It was funny how time passed quickly when you didn't want it to.

As the first star appeared Aragon approached him. He patted him on the shoulder. 'It's time,' he said. 'Our destiny calls.'

Omelette nodded.

Together they walked through the gathering dusk towards the farmhouse. The lights were on downstairs. Aragon fluttered up on to the windowsill.

He beckoned to Omelette. 'Look at this,' he whispered.

In the farmhouse the two brothers were playing cards. The kitchen table was covered in beer bottles. They were

both drunk. Snout sang a song. Against the grandfather clock were two guns. Suddenly Snout rose from the table and lurched towards the window. Omelette fluttered to the floor but Snout caught a glimpse of something.

'Somefink out there,' he said.

'Hide,' whispered Aragon.

They settled behind the water butt. The two brothers emerged with their guns in their hands. They stared about them into the gloom.

'See anyfink?'

'Nah! You must have imagined somefink, Snouty boy.'

'Saw somefink white, Harry. I swear it.'

'You was imaginin'. Here, was it pale and round?'

'Yer, it was, Harry. How you know?'

'It's the ghost with the floating head. Ain't you heard about him?'

Snout turned pale. 'Give over,' he said.

'It's sure to have been,' teased Harry. 'Floatin' ghosts all over the place – terrible frightening. You better watch out,' he said with a laugh.

The Old Man came out wearing a long white nightshirt and cap.

'What's all the noise?' he asked. 'Is it the fox?'

'Nah, nuffink, Dad. Snouty here fought he saw the floatin' ghost.'

The Old Man struck him across the back of the head.

'Here, what I do?' protested Snout, rubbing his head.

'Ghost?' said the Old Man. 'You're here to look out for that fox. If I lose any more chickens there'll be trouble.'

'Look, Dad, if you had a battery like I said you wouldn't have lost any.'

'Over my dead body. There'll be no batteries on my farm while I'm alive.'

'Yeah well, I'm only saying what I fink,' muttered Harry. 'No law against saying what you fink.'

'I'm the law here. Any more talk of batteries and I'll take the belt to you. Both of you! Now I'm off to bed.'

'Me too,' said Harry.

The Old Man turned on him. 'No bed for you, my boy. You stay up and look out for that fox and if I catch you snoozing there'll be trouble.' And the Old Man turned on his heel. The brothers waited until they heard their father going to bed and then they too went inside. From within came the chink of bottles.

'Perhaps if they're on guard we needn't stay,' whispered Omelette.

'They won't stay awake,' said Aragon, 'not with the beer they've drunk.'

Aragon was right. Within half an hour the lights went

97

on in the brothers' bedroom and soon loud and regular snores could be heard.

'Ready?' said Aragon.

'Ready,' Omelette said.

'I'll be over there in the lower branches of the oak tree. You stay here by the well. All you have to do is give the alarm. Don't do anything brave.'

'I'll do my best,' he whispered.

'Good luck,' said Aragon and patted him on the shoulder.

How funny life was, Omelette thought. Only a fortnight ago Aragon had been threatening to have him pushed down the well. Now here he was wishing him luck. He turned to speak but he had already disappeared into the night.

'Good luck,' whispered Omelette into the darkness. He shivered and crouched behind the well, making himself as inconspicuous as possible. In the barn an owl screeched and far away across the valley a church clock slowly struck twelve. Omelette's eyes strained into the dark. He could hardly see the outline of the oak tree, let alone Aragon. Pity there was no moon. He wouldn't be able to see the fox. But the fox wouldn't be able to see him either.

The wind rustled in the trees beside the fence. Like water rushing, Omelette thought to himself smiling. Then his heart stopped beating. There was no wind! The rustling continued. Where was it? There by the fence. Then he smelled it. That sharp bitter smell that could only mean one thing.

Fourteen

Silent as a phantom Monsieur Ricard loped across the yard. For the first time, as he passed through a shaft of light cast from Snout's window, Omelette saw him clearly; the half-nose eagerly sniffing the air, the thick brush floating behind. Omelette's throat felt dry. He tried to swallow but he couldn't. His whole body trembled with fear. He glanced towards the oak tree and wondered if Aragon had seen the fox. And if he had why had he not raised the alarm. What should he do? If he cried out he would give away his whereabouts and Ricard would be upon him in seconds. Why didn't the brothers wake up? He could still hear the snores emerging from the lighted window and ringing across the yard. Ricard heard them too. For a second he stopped and sniffed the air, then continued stealthily on his way.

Omelette wondered if he could reach the corrugated roof that led up to Snout's window. Once there he would be safe to sing out his alarm; to batter his body against the glass. Surely that would wake even the drunken and sleeping Snout. Ricard was once more in the shadows where Omelette could not see him but he could smell him. Slowly he began to creep across the yard towards the roof. He kept close to the hedge and skulked behind the tractor. Why hadn't Aragon given the alarm? Surely the fox was close to the tree by now. Omelette looked up at the

99

corrugated roof. Just a small jump and a flutter of the wings and he would be there. The smell of fox filled the night air.

Omelette whispered to himself: One, two, three! Then he half jumped, half flew upwards towards the roof. His claws scrabbled for a hold. For an awful second he thought he might fall and then he was there. Had Ricard heard the sound? He held his breath and listened. Silence.

He scrambled up the roof towards the window and pressed his beak to the glass. The curtains were open. Snout lay sprawled on his bed wearing only his pyjama bottoms. The gun lay across him pointing at the ceiling. With each snore his fat belly rose and fell. Softly Omelette tapped on the window. Snout continued to snore. Omelette tapped harder. But Snout was fathoms deep in drunken slumber. There was only one thing for it. Omelette gathered together all his strength and courage. With all the breath in his body he sang as piercingly loudly as he could and at the same time flung himself bodily against the pane of glass.

Snout was dreaming of the battery and how rich it would make him. In his dream he and his brother walked past line upon line of chickens. They were both dressed in top hats and white ties. There were thousands of chickens all piled higgledy-piggledy on top of one another in long narrow cages. And the eggs they laid were of gold! They poured into Snout's arms. He was knee deep in gold. He was rich. He saw himself on his private yacht beneath a sky of blue. A butler in a bow tie brought him a giant hamburger and a jug of lager on a silver tray, but when he raised the lager to his lips it suddenly changed into a pale and floating head. Its ears flapped horribly. There was a terrible crash. He screamed in terror and woke with a

100

start. It wasn't a dream at all. There *was* a head at the window. His nightmare had come true. The head was banging at the window. The window pane splintered and the head came through. It floated towards him. Its ears seemed to be flapping and from its mouth came the most horrible, frightening sound that Snout had ever heard. He screamed in terror, 'Help! Help! It's a floating head. Help me!'

Somehow his finger squeezed the trigger. The blast knocked Snout backwards on to the floor. The bullet blew a hole in the ceiling, and passed through the mattress on which the Old Man was peacefully sleeping, before exploding into the roof, where it brought a large lamp-shade crashing down on to his head.

The Old Man woke rather suddenly. His night cap was full of glass and ceiling plaster. He thought a great storm had struck the house. He leapt from his bed screaming, 'Hurricane, hurricane! Everybody out of the house!'

Aragon heard the violent commotion and began to sing as loudly as he could.

Meanwhile Omelette, frightened by the sudden gunshot, flew out of the window once more and rolled over and over down the corrugated roof. He wondered if he was wounded, yet he felt no pain. Perhaps he was already dead. He seemed to be rolling for ever. He saw the edge of the roof approaching and beneath it, to his horror, he caught a glimpse of the unmistakable outline of Monsieur Ricard.

By now Snout was clambering through the broken window in order to escape the floating head. He stood whimpering with fear on the corrugated roof. When he caught sight of Omelette rolling down the roof in front of him his whimpers turned into a scream of terror. And he let fly with the other barrel just as Omelette rolled off the roof and on to Monsieur Ricard below.

Monsieur Ricard was puzzled by the turn events had taken. Ten seconds earlier he had been creeping stealthily through the night, eagerly licking his lips in anticipation of the succulent chicken he would be taking home to his wife and cubs, when suddenly the whole farmyard had turned into a madhouse. A window splintered, there was an explosion followed by a flash of light that seemed to take half the roof off, a cockerel began to sing and three tail feathers fell on him. And then, to cap it all off, a featherless chicken chased by a half-naked man had fallen out of the sky. As if this wasn't enough there had been a flash of light followed by a loud explosion and his brush had left his body and floated away into the night. It was not what he was used to on a hunting expedition. Already he had lost his nose, now his tail, his most prized possession, was gone – bitten off, as far as he could judge, by a naked chicken that breathed fire. He knew when he was beaten. With a cry of pain and dismay he limped across the yard, under the gate and out across the potato field towards the safety of his lair. He trotted homewards vowing never to return.

In the light that now flooded the farmyard, the Old Man and his two sons staggered about blindly still trying to work out what had happened. Snout, the gun beneath his arm, wandered pale and shaking like one in a dream, muttering to himself over and over, 'The head! The head!'

His father tore the rifle from him.

'You could have killed me,' he shouted.

'Weren't me, Dad,' Snout mumbled pathetically.

'Not you! Who else would be so stupid? And who's going to pay for the roof?'

'But Dad . . .'

'Don't "Dad" me! What did I do to deserve this?' he shouted. 'Why couldn't I have had normal children like everybody else? You can stay out here till you learn some sense.' And so saying, he and Harry went back into the house bolting the door behind them.

Omelette crouched in the shadows. He heard a sound above him and looking up saw Aragon in the lower branches of the tree.

'A great victory, my friend.'

He fluttered down. Omelette was pleased to see him.

'What happened to your tail feathers?' asked Omelette.

'Dislodged in the assault, dear boy. *Wheee bang* and away they went!'

For a few moments they sat side by side in silence.

103

Then Omelette said, 'Were you frightened, Aragon?'

Aragon looked at him. 'Frightened?' he said. 'No. You?'

Omelette nodded. 'Yes, I was. Especially when I was waiting. When it all happened I didn't have time to feel anything.'

'The way you rolled off that roof on to the fox's back and bit off his tail while being shot at. Well, you deserve a medal.'

Omelette tried to explain what had really happened but Aragon would have none of it. 'Nonsense, you're just trying to be modest.'

Omelette was too tired to argue.

'Come on,' said Aragon, 'we'd best be back. They'll be wondering what's happened. What a story we'll have to tell, eh? What a yarn!'

And they set off tired but happy towards the hen coop. Suddenly Aragon turned back.

'Won't be a jiffy,' he said.

When he returned he was carrying Monsieur Ricard's brush.

'Just in case they don't believe us,' he explained.

'Spoils of war,' said Omelette, suddenly remembering Eric.

'For Morris,' said Aragon, waving the brush in the air.

'For Morris,' agreed Omelette.

The moon sailed out from behind a bank of cloud and bathed the valley in silver. The two warriors walked on in silence. Then Aragon stopped him.

'You know, you were asking me back there if I was frightened. Well, I was. Shall I tell you something else?' He hesitated and looked away. 'This is difficult to say,' he stuttered, staring at the floor. 'But when that Monsieur Ricard came to the hen coop . . .'

'When you were knocked out by the beam. And the others stopped you from going out and you were angry,' Omelette continued.

'Yes. Well, I was glad I was knocked out. And I was glad they stopped me too because it gave me an excuse for not going out and fighting him. Isn't that an awful thing?'

There was a long and profound silence. Aragon stared at the ground shamefacedly. Omelette said nothing.

'There's something else. I put you in the most dangerous place. I should have been near the well. But I was too frightened. That's a second awful thing.'

Aragon scratched at the dust with his claw and hung his head. 'Don't you despise me? Now that you know what I'm really like?'

Omelette embraced him. 'No,' he said, 'I like you better. It takes a lot of courage to admit you were frightened.'

Aragon perked up at this. 'Does it?' he said. 'D'you really think so?'

'Of course,' said Omelette. 'And you did have your feathers shot away. How many can say the same and live to tell the tale.'

'Tell the tale, that's a good one,' and Aragon swelled somewhat and recovered something of his former pride. 'By Jove, I think you're right,' he said.

'And you were *there*. If you'd been a real coward you wouldn't have gone at all.'

'That's true,' said Aragon. 'I *was* there.'

'And I was there.'

'We were there,' they both said in unison. And they grinned at one another and marched back to the hen coop singing:

'We were there, we were there . . .'

The singing got louder and louder but they didn't care who heard. They didn't care if the whole world heard.

At the hen coop they stopped.

'By the way,' muttered Aragon confidentially, 'no need to repeat what passed between us earlier about er . . .' and he tapped his beak with his wing, '. . . you know what.'

'Wouldn't dream of it,' said Omelette and together to hearty cheers from all the hens they entered the coop. Aragon waved Monsieur Ricard's brush triumphantly and the hens passed it from one to the other. Then Aragon told the story of the night's events. How Omelette had leapt from the roof on to Ricard's back and how Aragon had lost his tail feathers. It wasn't exactly how Omelette remembered it but the more Aragon repeated their adventures the less sure he became about what had actually happened. And he thought to himself, this is how history turns into legend.

And, back at the farmhouse, drenched and shivering, a pink figure clutched his pyjama trousers to him and hammered at the farmhouse door.

'Dad, Dad, let me in. Please, Dad, let me in!'

But no one heard except the silver moon that sailed bravely overhead.

Fifteen

After the great battle with Monsieur Ricard, life was better for Omelette. The hens treated him with a new respect and even Aragon, perhaps because of the adventures and the secrets they had shared, seemed to consider him as almost an equal. He began calling him by his real name instead of Ugly One or Bald One. He also seemed less boastful. It was as though his experiences in the battle had changed him. Omelette wondered if he too had changed. He decided it was much more difficult to detect changes in yourself than in others. And yet, when he thought about what he had been like when he had escaped from the van that night so long ago, there was no doubt that he *had* changed.

All this thinking about the past made him remember Eric and how he still missed him. A strange longing for his old home swelled up within him. 'Home,' he whispered to himself. He suddenly decided that the next morning he would set out. Life might be very pleasant with Aragon but there was really no place like your own home. It was going to be difficult explaining this to Aragon. His pride would be hurt but it had to be done. He decided to do it right away and set off across the farmyard in search of him.

On the way he caught sight of his reflection in a mirror that the brothers must have thrown out. He couldn't possibly set out with half his feathers missing. If he arrived home looking like that nobody would recognise him. He wondered if there was anything that could be done. He decided to seek a woman's advice.

Mercedes looked at him sympathetically as he explained his plight.

'My grandmother, bless her, always used to say that there was nothing like a roll in a wet dung heap for keeping the feathers up to the mark. But it has to be wet and sticky and you must keep it on for a day and a night.'

Omelette resolved to try and fortunately, later that morning a sudden downpour drenched the ground. He made his way to the dung heap and struggled to the top. Once there he began to daub himself from head to foot in the thick, smelly muck. Then he took a deep breath, counted three and rolled slowly from the top to the bottom gathering muck as he went. At the bottom he stood up with some difficulty because his head was still spinning. He looked like a ball of muck with legs. At the top were two small holes through which his eyes blinked anxiously. He wiped his beak. It was difficult to breathe and he smelled awful.

Sunbeam hurried by, head down, making for the shelter of the hen coop. She gave a squawk of terror when a small, round dung heap suddenly bowed and wished her 'Good morning'.

'Sunbeam, it's only me,' said Omelette, advancing towards her. Sunbeam backed away fearfully. 'Keep away, keep away from me, you horrible thing, or I shall scream,' she said, and then scurried for the safety of the hen coop screaming, 'Help, help, it's the bogeyhen!'

Feeling rather foolish, Omelette walked towards the hen house. By this time Mercedes had explained to

Sunbeam what was happening and she apologised to Omelette. The other hens were very polite and pretended there was nothing unusual about his appearance. The smell was a problem, though. They didn't exactly put their wings over their noses when talking to him but he did notice they kept their distance and held their breath for as long as they could. Despite the discomfort and the smell he kept the muck on for the rest of the night as Mercedes had instructed. That night he had plenty of room in which to sleep.

By the following morning the muck had set as hard as leather. Omelette experienced some difficulty getting to his feet. He had to walk with his legs and wings spread wide. Two or three times he fell over and the hens had to help him up. As she helped him up for the third time,

Mercedes remarked, 'Well, dear, you have to suffer for beauty.'

Omelette was longing to see if the cure had worked. He went to a quiet corner of the field and began to rub at the muck. But it wouldn't come off. He pecked at it. He rolled in the gravel. It was no use, nothing would shift it. Omelette wondered if it would ever come off. On balance he thought he would rather be bald than a walking dung heap.

'Why don't you take a dip in the duck pond, dear,' advised Mercedes from a safe distance through the swarm of flies that buzzed around Omelette. He set off, stiff-leggedly, for the duck pond. The flies followed.

The ducks were rather surprised to see a small bantam in a smelly overcoat doing the doggie paddle in their pond. He splashed and paddled vigorously for about half an hour.

When he finally struggled up the bank he rushed to the mirror, anxious to inspect his reflection. The muck had pretty well disappeared, but underneath he was as bald as he had ever been. He groaned aloud with dismay.

Sunbeam walked by. 'What are you looking so glum about?'

Omelette told her.

'I didn't think it would work. Why anybody in their right mind takes any notice of that Mercedes I shall never know. Now tell me, my sweet, do you really want your feathers back good as new?'

'More than anything,' said Omelette.

'Well, you listen to Sunbeam, lovey. Go down to the well and have a good soak in the water.'

'Will that make them grow?'

'Grow? I should cocoa. You won't be able to stop them.

That well's a holy well. Cure anything. Remember that frightful cough I had a week ago. What d'you think shifted it in the end?'

'Water from the well?' suggested Omelette.

'What else, my dear, what else!' she said, spreading her wings.

'I'll try it,' said Omelette decisively. After all, what had he got to lose?

He made his way towards the house where the well lay. It was the first time he'd been back since the battle. How different it all looked now in the calm of a sunny morning. Suddenly the back door opened and Omelette dived for cover behind the hedge. The Old Man came out carrying a laundry basket. He hung his nightshirt and night cap on the washing-line. Snout and Harry followed him. The Old Man was shouting at his sons.

'Well, tell them they can take them straight back.'

'But Dad,' protested Harry, 'I got the sheds and the hens at a special price – cheap rate, off this bloke I met in the pub.'

'Well, you'd better go and tell him to take them away again.'

'But he won't take them back. Even if he does you'll have to pay. That was the deal.'

'*I* won't have to pay. You'll have to pay. If you're stupid enough to buy things off strangers in pubs, that's your look-out.'

'*Dad!* I haven't got any money. This bloke'll kill me if I take 'em back.'

'That's your look-out. I told you, no batteries on this farm. Now get on with loading those bales. I don't pay you to sit around talking all day.'

The Old Man marched back into the house. His sons followed him still arguing.

111

For a moment the coast was clear. Warily Omelette crept towards the well. Beside it, tied with a rope, was a large galvanised bucket and a wooden ladle. Omelette scrambled up on to the stone parapet and peered down into the well. He couldn't see the water. It was very easy for Sunbeam to tell him to bathe in the well, but how was he to get down there? And more importantly, how was he to get out?

The heat of the morning sun had made him thirsty. He dipped his beak into the large bucket that brimmed with water, threw back his head and swallowed. Then a thought struck him. Of course, the bucket! That was water from the well. Why hadn't he thought of that before? He looked about him. The yard was deserted. Taking a deep breath he plunged into the bucket. The cold of it took his breath away. The water poured over the brim. Growing feathers seemed to be a very uncomfortable business, thought Omelette. Still, it would remove the rest of the smelly muck even if it did nothing else. He began to wash himself vigorously. The water discoloured slightly as the muck came off. He wondered how long he should stay in? Ten minutes? An hour? He began to swim in small circles to keep warm. As he swam he closed his eyes and began to daydream. He saw himself arriving home tired and bedraggled. Mrs Westmoreland ran out of the house to meet him, her arms outstretched . . .

'Did you hear him? Did you hear what he said?'

Omelette awoke with a start to see Snout and his brother Harry storming out of the farmhouse.

'He wouldn't do it, Harry. He wouldn't leave the farm to anybody else.'

'Wouldn't he?'

'We're his sons.'

112

'Yeah, but he doesn't treat us like sons, does he? We work like slaves every day of the year. When did we have a holiday? When?'

'I can't remember, Harry.'

'That's because we never had one. He pays us peanuts. We don't eat proper. The hens get better grub than we get. We don't even get Sundays off. And for what? For nothing. That's what. Just so he can leave the farm to somebody else when he feels like it! I'm not putting up with it. I've had it up to the throat with him.' Harry punched savagely at a pile of bales that was stacked on a trailer.

'Maybe you shouldn't have bought all them hens and that battery without asking, Harry.'

'Asking! Asking! It was a *fat accomplice*, Snouty. I was using my initiative, wasn't I? That's what you're supposed to do. If I'd have done that in the army they'd have given me the Victoria Cross. But not him. Oh no. What's he do? He says he's cut us out of his will. That's the reward you get off him. And another thing. What am I supposed to tell these blokes when they come round with all them hens and sheds this evening? *Can we have our money back please, mister?* They'll break both me legs. If not worse. I know these blokes.'

Harry slumped on the bales and groaned.

Snout looked round uncertainly. 'What you going to do, Harry?'

'I know what I'd like to do.'

'Load these bales?' suggested Snout.

'I'm not loading any bales. I'm not doing nothing more on this farm.'

'He'll go mad, Harry.'

'Let him. I want a drink of water.'

113

The two brothers walked towards the well. Omelette crouched low. What if they decided to lower the bucket into the well? They would be sure to discover him. Should he make a run for it now? But already it was too late. The two brothers sat on the wall of the well. Omelette could have touched them. He lay as low as he could in the bucket. Only his head was showing. He did his best to keep his beak from chattering.

'Pass us that ladle, Snout.'

A large tattooed hand almost brushed Omelette's head as Snout reached for the ladle. He sniffed it.

'Here, funny smell round here,' he said.

'If you ask me this whole farm smells. It smells of ingratitude,' said Harry, wiping the ladle on his shirt tail.

'Three thousand hens we could have had in them batteries. Three thousand. We could have been rich, Snouty. Rich beyond our wildest dreams.'

'Yeah, wildest dreams. Here Harry, talking of dreams right, the other night I was dreaming about what it would be like to be rich with lots of money. You wanna hear my dream, Harry?'

'No.'

'I was dreaming that we was living in this ginormous mansion, right. In the Souf of France, right. And like, in the wash-house instead of two taps there'd be three. One for cold, one for hot and one for lager. And outside there'd be like this enormous patio right, and in the middle a swimming pool in the shape of an hen. And everywhere there'd be these girls in bathing costumes bringing us tripe and pickled onion triple decker sarnies all day long.' Snout closed his eyes and sighed. 'It was beautiful, Harry, truly beautiful.'

'Yeah, well, you can forget about your dream. You

better start dreaming about sleeping in a cardboard box under a hedge 'cos that's what you're going to be doing from now on. It's either that or living a life of slavery.'

'What's he got against the battery, Harry?'

'He says it's cruel to the hens.' Harry snorted. 'Cruel to the hens! What a load of cobblers. How can you be cruel to hens? Hens ain't got no feelings.'

'Nah, hens ain't got no feelings, have they, Harry?' said Snout, coughing thickly and spitting between his boots.

'It ain't fair,' said Snout, slapping the ladle on the surface of the water. A tidal wave poured down Omelette's throat and into his eyes. He tried not to cough. For a moment the world spun round before his eyes.

'Here, give us a drink of that water.'

Without looking, Snout scooped a ladleful of water and passed it to Harry. Harry drank noisily and then spat out the water. 'Blimey, what's in this? Tastes like . . .'

He never finished the sentence. Just when Omelette thought he was bound to be discovered he heard another voice.

'What are you lazy, good-for-nothing layabouts doing? Do you think I pay you to sit around all day doing nothing and drinking my water?'

'Why don't you jump in a big hole and never come out,' said Harry under his breath.

'What did you say?'

'Nuffink, Dad,' said Harry.

'Nothing! That's all you're good for.'

'Dad, about these batteries. These blokes, they're coming round this evening and . . .'

'Don't you dare say another thing about those batteries. You so much as mention the word battery again in my hearing and you'll be off this farm tonight. . . Without a penny.'

'But, Dad . . .'

'You two will be the death of me one day. Now get on with these bales or do I have to take the belt to you?'

Snout leapt to his feet. 'Sorry, Dad . . .'

But Harry stopped him. He was smiling. 'That's it,' he whispered out of the corner of his mouth. 'You heard what he said. We'll be the death of him.' He looked at Snout. 'Are you thinking what I'm thinking, Snouty boy?'

Harry glanced up at the doorway high in the barn. Snout looked from the doorway back to his brother.

'What you mean, Harry?'

'I was just thinking, Snouty. Remember how that bale came off the 'ook and nearly killed me that time? Pity if it was to happen again, wouldn't it?' And he slowly winked one eye. 'Know what I mean, Snouty? Know what I mean?'

'Harry,' said Snout, going pale. 'You wouldn't.'

'No, *I* wouldn't but *we* would.'

'Me? It'd be murder, Harry.'

'Murder? What a nasty word, Snouty boy. I'd rather call it a haccident.'

'A haccident?'

'That's right. They happen all the time. Somebody is a bit careless with an 'ook and – Oh dear, poor old Dad happened to be standing right underneath the bale as it fell on him. What a terrible shame.'

Snout was trembling. 'I couldn't do it, Harry. Not murder.'

'And what was going to happen to me when these geezers came round for their money? What's sauce for the goose, Snouty. What about your dream?'

'Yeah, but . . .'

'Think about it. Souf of France. The swimming pools,

116

the girls, the food, the drink. All this could be yours, Snouty.'

'But . . .'

'Just do what I say,' said Harry.

They walked towards the trailer. The Old Man was slowly removing his belt.

'I've warned you before about sitting around when you should be working,' he said threateningly.

Harry spread his arms. 'Dad, I deserve it.'

The Old Man looked at him in astonishment. 'What!'

'You've been right all along, Dad. We can't even load these bales proper, can we, Snout?'

The Old Man looked at him in disbelief. 'Is this a joke?'

'A joke, Dad? Would I joke about something like this?'

Dark clouds rolled above the farm.

'Better get these bales shifted before the rain comes, Dad. If you could just show us how it should be done.'

The Old Man buckled on his belt again. 'Well, at least you've got the sense to ask my advice. Snout, you go up there and lower away.'

Snout's face was white with fear. 'Harry, I can't. I can't do it.'

'What d'you mean you can't?' said the Old Man. 'Get up those stairs and lower away or do I have to take my belt to you?'

'Don't hit me, Dad. Harry, don't make me do it. It was Harry's idea, Dad. Please.'

'Don't want to do what?' asked the Old Man suspiciously.

Harry snarled. Snout looked from one to the other. His knees trembled. 'Nothing, Dad. Nothing.' He almost fell.

'Are you feeling all right?' said his father, looking at him curiously.

'He's all right,' said Harry swiftly before Snout could answer. He slapped his brother on the back. Snout winced. 'It's something he had for his breakfast. We was just talking about it. Tripe and pickle sandwiches. He dreams about tripe and pickle sandwiches. But if he doesn't do what he's told he'll never have 'em again.'

'Pickle sandwiches? What are you talking about?' said the Old Man, his face going red with anger. He pointed. 'Now, you get up those stairs and hook up those bales or else!'

The thunder rumbled.

Snout made his way into the barn.

Omelette watched in horror. Could they really be going to murder their own father?

Snout stuck his head through the door and peered down, 'Dad, I . . .'

'Come on, hook it up and lower away,' ordered his father.

Meanwhile Harry pretended to ask for advice.

'It's just that I couldn't work out where to stand, Dad. Perhaps you could show me. If you wouldn't mind, that is. Then I'd know in the future.'

'Just stand to one side so it doesn't fall on you,' said the Old Man.

'Fall! That would be a terrible thing, wouldn't it, Dad? If one of them was to fall on you, I mean. I wouldn't be surprised if it killed you.'

The bale swung white and clear against the dark sky. The rope creaked and the bale spun slowly. Snout looked down his face as white as his shirt.

The thunder cracked. The two men looked up watching the bale. Suddenly the hook slipped.

'Look out, Dad!' screamed Snout.

Harry pushed his father who staggered sideways. Harry flung himself clear. The huge bale crashed down and struck the Old Man to the ground with a sickening thump. The sound echoed round the farm. The dust settled. There was a long and absolute silence. The world seemed to hold its breath. Even the birds had ceased singing. Lightning lit the three figures for an instant and thick drops of rain began to fall. Snout slowly descended the steps. He leaned on the doorway. Harry was crouching over the fallen figure.

'Is he. . . ?'

'Yeah. He's dead, all right,' said Harry. 'Dead as a stone.'

With a cry Snout fell to his knees. He began to sob uncontrollably. 'Dad, Dad, I didn't mean to do it. I didn't mean to, Dad. It was Harry. He made me. He made me.'

Harry lifted him to his feet. Snout wept hysterically. Harry slapped him hard across the face.

'Listen to me, Snout. Are you listening? It was an accident.'

'Yeah, an accident.'

'That's right. The hook slipped.'

'Yeah.'

'And now we're going for the police.'

'The police, Harry?'

'The police. We'll tell 'em what happened. That it was an accident. Understand? Leave the talking to me. You cry as much as you like but say it was an accident. Now come on.'

The two brothers disappeared round the side of the house. A few moments later their pick-up truck disappeared in a cloud of smoke, travelling in the direction of the village.

For a long time Omelette stood beside the well, staring at the scene but without seeing. He couldn't believe what had just happened. What creature would kill his own father? He felt sick. As if in a dream he made his way across the farmyard. It was noon but the sky was as dark as night. The rain fell on him but Omelette felt nothing. He shivered but it was not with the cold.

He stood before the other hens but for a long time he could not speak. When he finally managed to tell them what he had seen they wouldn't believe him.

'Kill their father? Nobody would do such a thing. You must have been having one of your dreams.'

But Omelette knew he had not been dreaming. He begged them to believe him. To quit the hut. He told them that the battery would be arriving that night. That they would all be locked up with thousands of other hens.

'You *must* sleep in the field tonight,' pleaded Omelette.

Aragon laughed. 'Me? Sleep in the field? In this weather? The very idea!'

Omelette left them. As he walked away the other hens looked at one another. One of them pointed at her head and nodded at the disappearing figure. 'I always thought he was a bit strange,' she said. 'Now I know.'

The other hens nodded wisely and settled down to sleep.

Omelette walked, not knowing where he was going. For a long time he sat staring at the river. Late in the afternoon a police car came and then an ambulance. They left and for a while there was silence.

Omelette did not return to the house but slept in a hollow by the river.

He did not see the three lorries that roared into the farmyard. Nor hear the sound of hammering.

In the morning Harry stood in the centre of the farm amongst the rows of sheds. He was wearing a new suit and was smoking a large cigar. As the sun rose he raised his hands to the sky and began to laugh and shout and dance for joy.

On a stone wall nearby sat Snout with his head in his hands. His shoulders heaved with sobs.

Inside one of the sheds Aragon awoke. It was time for him to rouse the sun; to sing his anthem to the morning. And yet it was still dark. He tried to move but three hens lay on top of him. He could not breathe. He scratched and pecked at the bars. But nobody came. Nobody ever came.

And Harry puffed on his cigar and looked round at what he had done and was pleased.

Sixteen

The next morning the sun was high in the sky when Omelette awoke from a terrible nightmare. He had dreamed that the two brothers had killed their father. He breathed a sigh of relief when he opened his eyes and saw the blue sky overhead. What ridiculous things dreams were! How good it was to see the sun shining and the green fields stretching about him just as they always did. He would be late for his singing lessons with Aragon. He shook and stretched himself into wakefulness, wondering why he had spent the night by the river. As he reached the brow of the little hill he called out, 'Aragon! Sorry I'm late, I . . .'

The words froze in his throat. Where the green meadow had once been there now stood rows of dark, squat sheds. The smell of sawdust and creosote filled the air.

Of the hens there was not a trace.

There was an awful silence. With a sickening shock Omelette realised that what he thought had been a nightmare had actually happened. Murder had been done in this place.

Warily Omelette crept up to the field and looked about. Nothing appeared to have changed and the brothers were nowhere to be seen. Stealthily he made his way towards the first of the sheds. In each one there was a small window covered in netting. Underneath in red was a painted skull and below it the message – 'KEEP OUT'. He peered inside, leaning his breast against the wooden wall. The saddest sight met his eyes; row upon row of hens crushed together one on top of the other in tiny boxes. Each box had wooden bars at the front. Those that could, stretched their necks through and pecked at morsels of seed that lay in a small trough. They seemed to be in a trance and made little noise. Omelette let his eyes wander along the rows of boxes. There was no one he recognised. He stepped back in dismay. The red skull had transferred to his chest but he didn't notice.

The same sight met his eyes at the next shed and the next. There must have been two thousand hens in all. Their eyes were dull and vacant. Many had plucked their feathers out and their necks were raw with rubbing against the bars. At each one he called out Aragon's name but no one answered. So dulled were the spirits of the hens that they hardly raised their heads at his call.

At the final shed he perceived the outline of a larger bird. If it *was* Aragon, he was dreadfully changed. His crop drooped and his shoulders were hunched in despair. His eyes were open but showed hardly any sign of life. Omelette scarcely recognised him.

'Aragon,' he called. 'Aragon, it's me, Omelette!'

Aragon's eyes swivelled but he showed no sign of recognition.

'Don't despair, Aragon. I'll do what I can to get you out of here.'

Aragon whispered hoarsely, 'There's no hope. No hope at all. Save yourself.'

'Aragon don't give up. I'll think of something.'

Aragon shook his head. 'There's nothing to be done. We should have listened to you. Goodbye, my friend, and good luck.'

Omelette walked between the rows of sheds and through the far hedge. Everywhere there was an unreal silence. The crows gathered in the treetops and it began to drizzle. He couldn't be bothered to run for shelter. He felt terribly alone. For the rest of the day he wandered aimlessly until, towards evening, he found himself in the yard at the back of the farmhouse. The rain had stopped and a sharp wind was blowing.

The sound of music drifted from the house. The light was on downstairs. Something made Omelette want to see the evil brothers. He knew he should have crept away but some strange force drew him to them. He crept towards the house.

Snout, wearing only his vest, underpants and socks, was sitting in a chair looking through a holiday brochure humming contentedly to himself. Harry was sitting at the kitchen table oiling a rifle. He wore his father's best suit. He snapped the rifle shut and squinted down the sight. Behind Omelette the branch of a crab apple tree creaked in a sudden gust of wind. Far off a vixen screeched.

Snout looked up nervously, ''Ere, what was that?'

'What?' asked Harry, giving the rifle a final polish.

'I fought I heard sumfink out there.'

Omelette held his breath.

'Just the wind, Snout, just the wind. Don't be nervous,' said Harry.

At that moment Omelette fluttered on to the windowsill and peeped in. His wing scratched the pane. Snout stood up and turned. Omelette hid behind the curtain. Snout threw down the brochure. His face was pale.

'There it is again. There *is* sumfink out there, Harry.' Snout's voice shook with fear. 'Maybe it's the floating skull, or, do you r . . . r . . . reckon it could be 'im, Harry?'

124

'Who?'

'Him! *His* g . . . g . . . g . . . ghost C . . . c . . . c . . .come back to get us, Harry.'

'No chance,' said Harry, 'he can't do nuffink to us. He's dead, Snouty Boy.'

'I know he's d . . . d . . .dead, Harry. We k . . . k . . .killed him. It's his g . . . g . . . ghost, Harry. Come back to haunt us. He's come back for r . . . r . . . r . . . revenge.'

'Don't be stupid.'

'It's true, Harry, don't m . . . m . . .mock. It's true. The dead come back. They come out of their graves and 'aunt the geezers what killed them. I read it in the paper.'

'Just let any ghost come near me, I'll let him have it,' said Harry, and he pointed the gun at the window and pulled the trigger.

The gun wasn't loaded but the click of the bolt made Omelette jump with surprise and he fell against the pane.

'Whassat?' cried Snout, his face turning white as paper.

'Whassat what?'

'Out there.'

The wind howled in the chimney.

'It's only the wind, Snouty, only the wind.'

'I thought I saw sumfink at the window, Harry. Sumfink white. Sumfink splashed with blood. Sumfink like a skull, Harry.'

Despite himself Harry was beginning to feel nervous. 'There's nuffink out there I tell you. It's all your himagination. Look, stop talking like that or you'll get me going.'

'I saw it, Harry. I saw it. A head all covered in b . . . b . . .blood.'

'No, you didn't. Go out and have a look. If you don't have a look you won't sleep tonight.'

'I don't fink I'll ever sleep again in my whole life, Harry.'

Furtively Snout opened the back door. The hinges creaked. He peered into the darkness. Omelette pressed himself flat against the window pane.

'Anyfink?' called Harry from inside the house. 'Any floating skulls yet?' And he laughed uproarously.

'Shurrup,' said Snout.

He crept into the yard. He could hardly breathe with fear. His heart thumped crazily. He looked about him, his eyes straining in the gloom. Nothing. His back to the house wall, like a climber on a cliff edge, he felt his way along. Something white and ghostly moved in the air. He gasped with fear but sighed with relief when he realised it was only washing on the line – his father's nightshirt and cap still hanging there. He inched along the wall towards the window feeling his way with outstretched hand.

Snout talked to himself to keep his spirits up. Fancy being scared of washing on the line. Harry was right. There were no such things as ghosts. And that noise. It probably *had* been the wind. What a fool he was making of himself.

He began to whistle tunelessly. Now he was at the window. His hand crawled slowly across the sill. Omelette watched it fascinated. It was as though he was hypnotised by the hand that moved towards him like a fat, white spider. He shrank back but it inched towards him, closer and closer.

In the kitchen Harry was beginning to feel nervous on his own. He loaded both rifles. It was very quiet. What if there *was* something out there in the night?

'Snout,' he called softly. 'Snout, are you there?'

But Snout didn't hear. He was feeling more cheerful. Ghost, he thought to himself, I'm not afraid of ghosts. He shifted another inch along the wall.

126

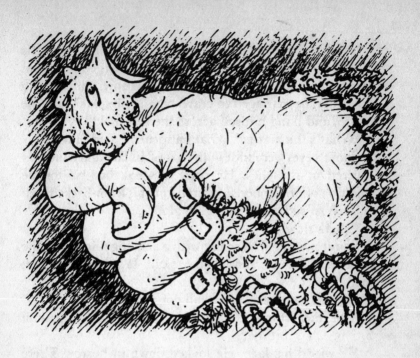

Omelette goggled at the moving hand his beak open, unable to move.

Harry called louder, 'Snout, you all right?'

As the word 'Yes' began to form itself on Snout's lips a great number of things happened very quickly one after the other. Snout's fat fingers closed on what he thought was a drain pipe. But it was thin and scrawny. The drainpipe was Omelette's neck. Snout felt the drainpipe gulp underneath his hand. There was a terrible shriek and the drainpipe bit him. Snout's 'Yes' turned into a spine-tingling scream which so startled Omelette that he flew scratching and pecking into Snout's face at which his screams re-doubled. Omelette who, if anything, was *more* frightened than Snout, fluttered away into the darkness screeching.

Snout seemed to have forgotten how to breathe. His face was yellow. Little moaning noises emerged from him and his lips drooled like a baby's. Somehow, whimpering piteously, he managed to crawl on all fours back into the house, and flung himself across the threshold.

'What's the matter? What happened?' said Harry.

Snout's eyes were wide with terror. His face and hand was covered in scratches. He tried to speak but his tongue wouldn't obey. Gibberish poured from his foam-flecked lips.

'Dah su su kll ugh ugh glob glob . . .'

'Speak slowly.'

Snout pointed frantically with a shaking finger into the darkness. 'The sk. . .sk. . .sk. . .skull. It g. . .g. . .g. . .got me.'

'How d'you mean, the skull got you?'

'Got me, Harry. It got me. The s. . .s. . .s. . .skull b. . .b. . .b. . .bit me.'

He wiped his face. He looked down in horror. There was red paint on his hand and face.

'*Aaaaaaah!*' he screamed. 'B. . .b. . .b. . .blood. I'm dying, Harry. I'm dying. The sk. . .sk. . .skull bit me.'

Harry looked out through the open door. All seemed to be quiet. He took a long swig from the whisky bottle. 'I'm going to sort this out once and for all. I'm not scared of ghosts. I'm not scared of nuffink.'

He released the safety catch on his rifle and walked towards the door.

'You coming with me? Or you going to lie there like a coward?'

Snout crawled across the kitchen floor. He clung to Harry's leg, dragging him almost to the ground. 'Don't leave me on me own, Harry. I'm coming, Harry, I'm coming. Don't leave me.'

Harry shook him off.

He picked up a torch. 'Bring the other gun and don't do nuffink unless I tell you.'

Rifle to his shoulder Harry emerged into the darkness. He shone the torch into the corner of the yard. Snout crawled behind him clinging to his coat, carrying the second rifle. Slowly the beam of light swept across the yard.

Omelette was sitting by the well, trying to recover from the fright Snout had given him. He saw the torchlight and Harry silhouetted in the doorway cradling a rifle in his arms. Slowly the triangle of light moved towards him. Soon he would be in its beam. But there was somebody or something else out there in the darkness. Something he couldn't see but somehow knew was there. Perhaps there were such things as ghosts. He heard a rustling at his back. His head whipped round. Nothing! Had Snout somehow got behind him? No, there he was skulking and gibbering behind his brother. Again he heard a rustling in the undergrowth. There *was* somebody there! Again he looked round and to his horror made out an indistinct figure, white and gleaming in the darkness. Its eyes glittered.

'Who's there?' he whispered hoarsely.

'Omelette?' whispered the voice.

'Yes. Who is it? How did you know my name?'

'Never forget a name, Omelette.'

The figure moved closer. Omelette cowered.

'Especially the name of a friend,' said the ghost.

Closer and closer came the ghostly figure. Omelette's eyes strained into the darkness. It had a straggly beard and horns.

'Eric!' cried Omelette. 'The ghost of Eric!'

129

'The same,' said Eric.

'Have you come to haunt me?'

'Haunt you? Why should I haunt you?'

'You are a ghost, aren't you?'

'Not as far as I know,' said Eric.

'But you're dead. You drowned in the river.'

'Well, it was very nasty for a moment. But this is me, all right. Touch.'

Omelette touched the hard forehead. That was solid enough. And warm.

'It's really you. And you're alive!' he cried joyfully.

'Alive? I should think so. Don't think I'd be walking about like this if I was dead, do you?'

Suddenly the beam of a flashlight illuminated Omelette.

'There it is,' whispered Snout hoarsely, pointing a trembling finger at Omelette. 'The bleeding skull!'

At the sound of the voice Omelette flung himself sideways. Harry squeezed the trigger and a foot of flame leapt from the nuzzle of the rifle. There was a huge explosion and the bullet tore a smoking groove in the ground, throwing clods of grass into the air where just a second earlier Omelette had been sitting.

'Missed him,' cursed Harry. 'Where's it gone?'

Eric was beside Omelette now. 'Looks as though you're in some kind of trouble?' Eric said calmly.

'Yes,' said Omelette. 'They're trying to shoot me.'

'So they are, so they are,' said Eric softly. 'Only one answer to that. I think a little charge is called for. Leap aboard.'

In one swoop Omelette was up on Eric's back. He reared terrifyingly in the dark.

'Charge!' shouted Eric.

'Charge!' yelled Omelette.

Eric lowered his head and pawed the ground. Then he was thundering across the yard straight at the brothers with all the power in his mighty body.

Snout couldn't believe his eyes. 'What's that?' he screamed.

What he saw in the faint light of the torch was a tall, bearded figure topped by a swaying red skull that galloped, swaying eerily towards them. And the skull was crowing. It has been known for people to die of fright. Snout was at this moment very close to this.

'It's got hooves,' screamed Harry.

'A bleeding skull with hooves.'

'It's the Devil!' screamed Harry, firing desperately at the hurtling figure. The bullet split the washing-line bringing the Old Man's nightshirt fluttering down just as Omelette was passing underneath. It draped itself about him and fell over Eric's eyes.

'I can't see,' yelled Eric.

'Charge!' screamed Omelette, the nightshirt sliding down his neck. Eric galloped blindly on.

When they finally hit the patch of light what Harry and Snout saw was a ghostly blood-red skull dressed in his father's fluttering nightshirt under which could be seen pounding hooves. Snout screamed. He stumbled backwards. 'It's the Old Man's skull in his nightshirt.'

'Charge!' shrieked Omelette.

'A glrrgh mgggh splat goroboo,' said Snout.

'Charge!' shouted Eric, gathering speed.

'Let's get out of here!' screamed Harry.

But it was too late. Eric was upon them. Snout tried to scramble to his feet, but the barrel of the gun had become inextricably entwined in the elastic of his underpants. The

131

other barrel went off. The shot scorched across his backside ripping the elastic on his underpants. They fell about his ankles and he collapsed once more.

Eric's horns picked up Harry and rolled and butted him round the yard. The torch fell to the floor and the light went out. Eric turned on Snout who found himself upside down in mid-air with a terrible pain in his backside. He landed with a crash on his back and looked up to see a horned creature with a beard and piercing eyes standing over him. His tattered underpants fluttered from one horn like a flag. Snout knew he was looking into the face of the Devil. And then before his amazed eyes a red skull floated eerily from the body and descended on him like a fury.

Eric began to bundle the two brothers, tossing them like rags about the yard. Stumbling and screaming they finally reached the door. But Eric was not finished with them yet. Through the house he chased them, through the kitchen, down the hall through the front door and down the path. At the garden hedge Eric stopped. The two friends laughed as they watched the two brothers disappear over the distant hill, Harry still clutching his foot and hopping and Snout trying unsuccessfully to hold his vest over his wobbling and tender bottom.

Then they were gone.

'I don't think we'll see them for a while,' said Eric.

'No,' said Omelette. 'Good riddance to bad rubbish.'

There was a silence as the two friends looked at one another happily.

'What are you thinking about?' asked Eric.

'That I'm glad you're still alive.'

'Yes,' said Eric, 'I'm quite pleased about that too.'

There was another silence.

They walked back into the house. A log fire burned in

132

the grate. Eric settled himself comfily on the sofa. Omelette in the armchair.

'I've got a story to tell,' said Omelette.

'So have I,' said Eric.

'Me first,' said Omelette.

The two friends smiled at each other in the firelight.

And Omelette told his story while the logs crackled in the hearth and the moon hung silent in the frame of the window. So still that you might have thought that he too was listening.

Seventeen

'Well, that's my story. Now you must tell me yours.'

It was after midnight and Omelette had been talking for hours. The embers shifted in the grate and Eric nodded. He had listened, fascinated. Every now and then he had asked a question but most of the time he simply sat and listened. Now it was his turn.

'Start with when the bridge broke,' said Omelette.

'As I felt the bridge breaking underneath me I thought I was gone. I hung on for as long as I could and then let myself go. Fortunately the river was deep where I fell. I seemed to sink for ever. I thought I was never going to reach the surface but then I was thrown clear. I tried to swim but the current was so strong it swept me along. Anyway goats aren't noted for their swimming. The main dangers were the rocks and boulders. I don't know how far I was carried. I didn't have time to look at the bank, I was too busy trying to keep myself afloat. Eventually I found myself turning round and round, faster and faster and being sucked down. I realised I was in a whirlpool. There was no point in fighting. Down and down I went. I held my breath for as long as I could but then I could hold it no longer. I remember longing for good clean air. The last thought that went through my head was, "I'm going to drown". Then everything went black.

'I don't know for how long I was unconscious. It might

have been days. But when I came to I was in utter darkness. I couldn't see my hoof in front of my face and my head was aching terribly. I must have hit a rock. My leg ached terribly, too. I climbed to my feet and stumbled a few paces and came upon a rock wall. Then I walked back in what I thought was the opposite direction and came against another wall. I realised I must be in some sort of cave. The question was, which was the way out? I began to walk in the direction of what I thought was the mouth, but then I met water and it became deeper and deeper. I could go no further. I realised I was walking towards the river. The whirlpool must have thrown me up into an underwater cave. I turned about and returned the way I had come.

'I seemed to walk all day and it was with the greatest of pain. I began to see spots in front of my eyes. Then the spots became one spot. It got bigger and bigger. To my delight I realised it must be daylight. Then I saw green fields. A tree. A patch of sky. I began to trot, forgetting my injured ankle. For a few steps I didn't notice the pain. Then I began to limp again — but I didn't care, it was so wonderful to see the sunlight. And then I was out in the air with the grass beneath my hooves once more. It dazzled me. I looked about me and saw rows of eyes peering at me. What they were I didn't know. My eyes were still dazzled by the brightness. And then everything went black again.'

'But how did you find me?' asked Omelette.

'Patience, my friend. I don't know for how long I slept but when I woke up I found myself in the mouth of the cave on the side of a mountain with four or five goats looking down on me. I told them my story and said I must find my friend.'

'You said that?' said Omelette proudly.

'Yes, but they didn't want me to go. "You must stay here until you are rested and your injuries are healed," they said.

' "But I am rested," I told them, "I have no injuries." I tried to get to my feet but I couldn't. The pain in my leg was terrible. I must have hit a rock while I was in the river. It took a long time for it to heal. At first I lay in the mouth of the cave, not moving. The other goats brought me grass. Later I was able to get to my feet; then to walk a little. Gradually my strength returned. At last I felt fit enough to continue my journey.'

'I thought you had drowned,' interrupted Omelette. 'I thought you were dead.'

'That's what I thought,' replied Eric.

'But how did you manage to find me?' asked Omelette.

'I'm just about to tell you,' said Eric, smiling at the little bantam's impatience. 'The goats led me to the river and there we said our farewells.

'I began to walk upstream. I thought the one thing I was certain of was the broken bridge and the whirlpool. That would give me a starting point. To tell you the truth I didn't have very high hopes of finding you. I walked for the best part of a day and saw nothing familiar. I even wondered if I was walking beside the right river. Then I saw something.'

'What was it?'

'A feather.'

'But there are lots of feathers.'

'This was a special feather. The feather of a golden eagle. Not only that, it was stuck into a pile of small stones.'

'That was our feather,' said Omelette. 'I put it there on your grave.'

'Is that what it was?'

'Sort of. And to remind me where you'd died.'

'You did that for me?' said Eric.

'Did it feel funny looking at your own grave?'

'Well, I didn't know that's what it was at the time. I thought it was a sign.'

'Well, carry on.'

'I'm trying to, but you keep interrupting.'

By now the fire was nothing but glowing ashes. They shifted closer to its warmth. Through the window the sky was turning from black to grey.

'I won't say another word,' said Omelette.

'Well, I looked up and saw the whirlpool and then further upstream the cliff and the broken bridge hanging off it, so I knew I was in the right place, but I didn't know what to do next. I'd found the place where you'd seen me last but that didn't really help. So I just wandered along the riverbank looking for signs. And then I saw one.'

'What was it? A claw print? A broken branch? A . . .' Omelette hesitated. 'Sorry! Carry on.'

'None of those things. Something much better.'

'What?'

'A feather.'

'A feather?'

'But not an ordinary feather. One of yours. I walked on a few paces then I found another and another. I thought how clever of him. He's plucked out his feathers one by one and left them as a trail for me to follow. Well, I followed the trail . . .'

'Excuse me, Eric, I know I said I wouldn't interrupt again but I have to tell you something. I didn't pull out my feathers to leave a trail, they just fell out.'

'Fell out?'

137

'On their own. Hadn't you noticed I was bald?'

'Well, I had as a matter of fact. And I also wondered why you had a skull in red paint on your chest.'

'I leaned on some red paint that was still wet. That was what frightened the brothers. But what happened when I got in the boat? You wouldn't be able to find the feathers on the river.'

'Ah, so that's what happened. Well, when the feathers stopped suddenly on the edge of the river I thought something like that must have happened. I crossed to the other side by another small bridge and then, a bit further down, followed the feathers up the hill and the next thing I knew I heard a gun going off and I was in the middle of a battle.'

'Which we won,' said Omelette.

'We did indeed. Didn't they run when they saw the nightshirt!'

They both began to laugh. Omelette realised that it was a long time since he'd laughed like that, 'I'm glad you're back, Eric,' he said. 'It wasn't the same without you.'

'Me too,' said Eric. They smiled at one another. The fire was out now and the sun was glinting through the farmhouse window. The thought struck Omelette that he should be helping Aragon with his singing. But then he suddenly remembered Aragon was locked up. So were all the other hens. He would never sing again. He turned to Eric.

'How are your hooves?'

'My hooves? Fine. Why?'

Omelette strode out of the door.

'Where are we going?' asked Eric.

'I've a job for you,' said Omelette.

In the field all was quiet. Omelette walked up to the first shed.

'Would you kick this door down for me, please.'

'Who's inside?'

'Some friends of mine.'

'Make way,' said Eric.

He turned his back on the door, put his head down and flung out his back legs. The door splintered and then swung free. From within came anxious murmurs. The two entered. A hundred bewildered eyes stared at them out of the gloom. At one end of the row of cages was a long bar.

'If we pull this all the cages will be opened,' said Omelette.

Eric gripped it in his teeth and pulled it. He pulled it until he was out in the field. The hens didn't move.

Already their spirits were accustomed to being locked up. Omelette walked along the shed shouting at them. Eric rattled the cages. One by one the hens lifted the barred doors and dropped down on to the floor. Nervously they walked out into the sunlight, blinking anxiously.

'Now the others,' said Omelette.

Soon all the hens were free. There seemed to be thousands of them. They walked and clucked about the field as if they had never seen grass or sunshine before. Some wandered into the house. They began to pull at the stuffing in the sofas and chairs and in the mattresses upstairs; they ate the grain in the barn; they raided the pantry and ate the bread and butter and biscuits. They were everywhere.

In the last shed was Aragon. When he saw Omelette he was lost for words.

'I don't know what to say . . . I . . . look . . . here . . . I say . . . my goodness,' he stuttered. There were tears in his eyes.

'No need to say anything. I understand,' said Omelette.

They walked out into the field. Aragon gazed about him. 'All these hens,' he said smiling. 'And all mine!'

'I have a suggestion,' said Omelette.

'Anything, dear boy, anything.'

'Why don't you sing?' he said.

'Sing?'

Omelette shrugged. 'It just seemed appropriate. To sort of celebrate our victory and your freedom. Of course if you don't want to . . .'

'What d'you mean "don't want to"? Have you ever known me turn down an invitation to sing?'

Aragon stood on tiptoe, thrust out his shimmering golden chest, filled his lungs and sang a song the like of

140

which neither Omelette, nor Eric, nor the hens, nor anyone who was fortunate enough to be passing on that famous day had ever heard before. The glorious sound cannoned off distant cliffs and exploded in the skies. On and on it rolled like an unstoppable, multicoloured torrent. It curled and weaved and turned back on itself. It was peppered with arpeggios and threaded with rolling rallantandos. And then with a final soaring coda it was over.

'Thank you,' said Omelette at last.

'Least I could do, dear boy.'

'What will you do now?' asked Eric.

Aragon stroked his chin. 'Thought I might stay here. Those scoundrels won't be back, will they?'

'Not for a bit. But some time they'll come back. I wouldn't stay too long if I were you.'

'Ah! Point taken. Well, perhaps we'll move on. You coming with us?'

'No. Not this time,' said Omelette, throwing a glance at Eric. 'There's somewhere we have to find.'

Eric nodded.

'Quite,' said Aragon. 'Well, I'll say goodbye.' He saluted smartly.

The three of them, Aragon, Eric and Omelette marched solemnly across the field side by side. The hens gathered about them. They were whispering something. The whispering grew until all were chanting in unison. Omelette couldn't quite make out what it was.

'What's that they're saying?' he asked Aragon.

'They've given you a new name.'

'Me?' said Omelette.

'After your victory. They want you to know that they're grateful.'

'What is the name?' The hens had called him many names in the past. Mainly they had been insulting ones.

'Brave Red Skull.'

Omelette didn't know what to say. He moved through the ranks of assembled hens murmuring, 'Thank you, thank you, very kind of you.' In his heart, though, he preferred the name Omelette but it didn't seem polite to say.

They reached the front of the house. It was time for farewells.

'Goodbye,' said Omelette.

'Perhaps we'll meet again, some day.'

'I'll hear from you anyway,' said Omelette.

'Hear?' said Aragon, frowning.

'The singing,' said Omelette.

'Ah. You mean the voice. I'll put in a special little tra-lah-lah, just for you. Listen out for it.'

'I shall,' said Omelette. 'I might even reply. Of course I won't be in the same class as you, but I'll do my best.'

'Of course not,' said Aragon and then remembered that he was trying to be modest. 'Oh, I don't know,' he said with a shrug of his shoulders.

Omelette saluted him once more. 'We'll be on our way.'

They walked down the lane.

'I say,' called Aragon.

Omelette stopped and turned.

'Keep an eye on your tail,' he said with a wink.

'Tail?' said Omelette. 'What d'you mean?'

'You'll find out. Just do as I say.'

Eric and Omelette walked across the farmyard, through the gate and down the lane. At the bottom of the hill they turned and looked back. Aragon was standing on the top of his dung heap. His feathers shimmered in the morning sunlight. Sharp, stacatto instructions filled the air. The hens were lined up in three ranks. At a command from Aragon they marched past the dung heap, their eyes raised towards him.

'Like a General,' said Eric.

'An Emperor,' said Omelette.

Aragon's song filled the air. It was a marching song of Freedom. The columns of hens marched briskly out of the farm and down the valley. At last they were gone.

'Come on,' said Omelette, descending the hill. He would miss Aragon. He thought about the last words he had said to him. Something about keeping his eye on his tail. That was a strange thing to say.

Without looking round he said, 'What d'you think he meant when he said I was to keep an eye on my tail?'

Eric laughed. 'I know what he meant, all right.'

'What?'

'Take a look,' said Eric.

Omelette stopped. On his tail, soft down had appeared. It was on his wings too and his neck.

'My feathers,' he exclaimed. 'Eric, my feathers, they're starting to grow again. I hadn't noticed.'

'So they have,' said Eric.

They gazed over the landscape. The river winding through the valley. The cloud of yellow gorse on the hillside. They both breathed deeply and looked at one another.

'Are you going where I'm going?' asked Eric.

'I think so,' said Omelette.

'Home?' said Eric.

'Home,' agreed Omelette. 'Any idea which way?'

Eric nodded East and towards the river.

'This looks as good a way as any.'

And together the two friends descended into the valley.

Eighteen

After three weeks of searching, hunger finally brought them down into a lakeside village. On the green was a large red and white striped marquee. Outside on a low platform a brass band was playing. One side of the marquee adjoined an overgrown field. The two travellers crept through the long grass until they stood close to the tent. A large sign on the side said:

AMBERSLEY & DISTRICT
HORTICULTURAL & LIVESTOCK
SUMMER SHOW.

A crowd of people marched past led by a young woman in a red beret. She carried a placard that said:

STOP CRUELTY TO ANIMALS.
ANIMALS DESERVE LIFE AND FREEDOM
TOO!

The young woman climbed on to a box and began to make a speech. A crowd gathered round. Some of them laughed. Many shouted and booed. The young woman carried on speaking. The more people shouted the better she seemed to speak. Two men at the back threw ripe tomatoes. They exploded against the placard and the crowd laughed and cheered even louder. The girl in the red beret shook her fist at the men and shouted at them.

The crowd applauded her. There was something about her. Omelette felt sure they'd met before but he couldn't remember where. He racked his brain but it was like trying to see somebody in a fog. Eric's voice brought him back to the present.

'Leeks!' he exclaimed. 'I can smell leeks.' His nose was in the air and he was sniffing ecstatically. 'Come on,' he said, 'let's sneak into the marquee.'

'What if we're caught?' said Omelette.

'What difference will it make? We've been looking for our home for weeks without any luck. Suppose somebody does catch us? They may adopt us. Anything's better than wandering those hills in the wind and the rain with only grass to eat.'

'That's all right for you but what happens if we go to a farm where they make us disappear? I don't want to . . .'

Suddenly Omelette stopped speaking. He too raised his nose and sniffed the air. A wonderful smell circled him and drifted into his nostrils. He closed his eyes and sighed a long sigh.

'Food!' he said. 'I can smell food.'

They crouched down and lifted a flap of the tent and peered inside.

A number of contestants were putting the final touches to their exhibits. There were tables filled with huge apples and potatoes and tomatoes and leeks and every fruit and vegetable imaginable. Nearest to them were cages with rabbits, hens, dogs and cats in them. Their owners stroked and brushed them carefully.

'Leeks,' said Eric, licking his lips, 'just look at the size of those leeks. And carrots.'

They were about to enter beneath the flap when a pair of strong, stockinged legs in brown brogues approached

145

them. They dodged back under the tent and squinted upwards. The owner of the legs opened a cage and stroked a fat brown hen.

'Buffy Poohs, my beautiful one,' she cooed, 'didn't you win a nice prize for Mummy? Yes, you did. Here's some more nice seed for you, darling.'

'That's what I could smell,' whispered Omelette, 'those seeds.'

Outside the band began to play a stirring march and the crowd cheered. A large black shiny car drew up. Out of the car strode a tall man in a grey suit. The lady in the brogues clapped her hands and everybody inside the tent went quiet.

'Ladies and gentlemen,' she said in an excited voice, 'I hear the band. That means our dear Lord Dalrymple has arrived. Would everybody please go to the platform on the Green. Lord Dalrymple will make a short speech and then return to give the winners their prizes. So everybody out of the tent, please.'

There was a buzz of excited conversation and all the people walked out of the tent. A few moments later Lord Dalrymple began to speak into a microphone.

The young woman in the beret shouted at him but the crowd turned around and told her to keep quiet. She carried on shouting but Lord Dalrymple had a microphone so her cries weren't heard.

'Come on,' said Eric, 'now's our chance.'

He dodged under the flap followed by Omelette. Eric began to eat the prize leeks. When he got tired of them he moved on to the carrots. Then he ate one of the rosettes. 'Very tasty,' he murmured between mouthfuls.

Omelette looked up at the cage containing the large brown hen. Beside her was a pile of seeds. She pecked at them nonchalantly.

'Hello,' said Omelette.

The fat hen was wearing a blue satin sash over her shoulder to which was pinned a red rosette. She looked down at him disdainfully and turned away.

'Those seeds look jolly nice,' said Omelette, smiling. 'Jolly nice.'

The hen ignored him. There was a tearing sound. Eric had started on the tablecloth.

Omelette looked back at the hen. On her cage was a printed sign. It said:

DOMESTIC FOWL–BUFF ORPINGTONS
BUFFY POOHS
SUPREME PRIZE
BEST BIRD IN SHOW

Underneath was written the owner's name. 'Miss Edna Tudno Watkins'.

'Excuse me,' said Omelette to the hen, 'we've been wandering in the hills for weeks. We're trying to find our home but I don't know if we ever shall. You get jolly hungry up in the hills. Just grass, you see. No seeds at all.' The brown hen carried on eating. 'No seeds at all,' repeated Omelette a little more loudly.

The Buff Orpington looked down her beak at him.

'Go away,' she said loftily.

'I only want a few,' said Omelette. 'I'm starving. It's all right for Eric, he can eat grass, but I'm starving and it looks as though you have more than enough there.'

'You've got a cheek even speaking to me. Don't you realise I'm a Supreme Champion? What breed are you?'

Omelette shook his head. 'Dunno,' he said.

'Every bird who is *anybody* has a breed and an owner. My owner is Miss Tudno Watkins. She's very proud of

147

me.' She carefully adjusted the sash. 'Now go away, it could spoil my chances if I'm seen with the likes of you.' And she turned her back on Omelette.

'Having trouble?' said a voice. It was Eric.

'I only wanted a few seeds and she won't let me have any,' said Omelette.

'I see,' said Eric. He turned to the cage. 'Here you, Buffy Poohs, or whatever your name is!'

The Buff Orpington looked Eric up and down as though he were a slug she couldn't be bothered to eat. 'Lawks,' she said. 'A smelly goat. Whatever next!'

Eric ignored the insult. 'I believe my chum here asked you for some seed,' he said in his politest voice. 'Now it looks to me as though you have more than enough for yourself, so I think it would be a courtesy to throw a few his way.'

'I'm going to be introduced to a Lord any minute now so why don't you improve the quality of the air in this tent by going outside.'

Eric heaved a sigh. 'Oh dear, oh dear, I didn't want this to happen. I asked you politely. I gave you a chance. Now I'm afraid I'm going to have to insist.'

With his nose he undid the catch on the cage and began to shake it.

'Put me down. How dare you!' screamed Buffy Poohs angrily.

Eric shook the cage harder. The Buff Orpington fluttered clumsily to the floor in a mass of feathers and outrage.

'Now clear off!' Eric chased the protesting hen across the ground. She scuttled squawking out under the flap.

From the platform outside came a burst of clapping. Lord Dalrymple had finished his speech.

'They're coming back!' hissed Eric. 'Hide!'

But Omelette didn't hear him. He was sitting in the Buff Orpington's cage gulping down seed as fast as he could go. He had never tasted such delicious food.

Lord Dalrymple entered the marquee accompanied by Miss Edna Tudno Watkins and the other contestants.

Eric disappeared under one of the tables. Omelette hadn't noticed the crowd approaching. He was too busy eating.

Miss Tudno Watkins walked backwards bowing to Lord Dalrymple. They walked along the line of exhibits. At each one, his Lordship stopped and shook the hand of the winner as he gave out the prizes. Each time the crowd clapped.

Eventually they reached the cage in which Omelette was sitting. He was getting to the bottom of the pile of seeds. His head was deep in the cup and his back was turned towards the dignitaries.

'Here she is,' cried Miss Edna Tudno Watkins, who still had her back to Omelette, 'my beautiful Buffy Poohs. Oh, I'm so proud of her.'

Lord Dalrymple peered through his monocle. He saw a rather small, moth-eaten bantam who had his head plunged into a pot of seeds. His backside pointed at Lord Dalrymple. Omelette was so engrossed in his eating that he noticed nothing. Then quite suddenly he did something that one is not supposed to do in front of lords of the realm.

'Good heavens!' cried Lord Dalrymple in astonishment, and his monocle slipped from his eye. He began to rub at his suit with his handkerchief.

'What happened?' said a red-faced farmer.

'It was the Buffy Poohs,' said a thin lady in a white straw hat, 'he did a number twos.'

'What? In front of his Lordship?' said the other in astonishment.

'Over him,' said the lady in the white hat.

His Lordship replaced his monocle and stared at Omelette.

'What is this?' he enquired frostily.

Miss Edna Tudno Watkins turned round. When she saw Omelette her mouth dropped open.

'Buffy Poohs, what has happened to you? Where are your lovely feathers?'

Omelette looked up for a moment and then carried on with his meal.

'Is this some kind of joke?' asked Lord Dalrymple. 'If it is, it's in extremely poor taste.'

'That's not Buffy Poohs,' cried Miss Edna Tudno Watkins. 'She's been stolen. Kidnapped. Who's stolen my

Buffy Poohs? Send for the police! Nobody leave the marquee!'

She began to shake the cage savagely. 'You villain!' she screamed at Omelette. 'What have you done with my darling Buffy Poohs? You savage! You kidnapper!'

Omelette, full of seed, rolled around the cage in some bewilderment.

By this time some of the other prize winners had discovered the ragged remains of their carrots and leeks.

'Some vandal has been at my leeks,' shouted the red-faced farmer. 'Who is it? Come on. Own up.'

The crowd began to scream. Miss Tudno Watkins battered the cage with her umbrella. It fell to the ground with Omelette still inside. He cried out with fear. She began to kick the cage across the floor screeching with anger. It rolled over and over. Omelette rolled with it.

The girl in the red beret burst through the crowd still carrying her placard. When she saw what was happening to Omelette she advanced on Miss Edna Tudno Watkins.

'How dare you ill treat that poor bantam,' she shouted.

Miss Tudno Watkins turned on her. Her face was puce and her eyes bulged angrily.

'How dare you speak to me like that. You, you rabble rouser. Don't you realise who I am! I am the chairlady of the district Poultry and Egg Society. Now leave this tent at once. You have no business here you, you, you Communist you. You criminal.'

'It's you who's the criminal,' said the girl in the beret. 'You pretend to love animals but really you hate them.'

'Oh my goodness,' blustered Lord Dalrymple. 'Stop this unseemly behaviour.'

But Miss Tudno Watkins had completely lost her temper. She advanced on the young girl like a ferocious bull, swinging her umbrella round and round her head. It caught the young girl a glancing blow.

'How dare you hit me,' shouted the girl, 'how dare you?' She raised the placard above her head and brought it down with all her might over Miss Tudno Watkins's head. There was an awful splintering sound as her head tore through it. The crowd screamed. One or two of the young girl's followers applauded and shouted, 'Give it to her, girl!'

Lord Dalrymple cried, 'Ladies, ladies. Please! Somebody call the police!' He wrested the placard from the young girl and tried to lift it from Miss Tudno Watkins's head. It stuck under her chin. Lord Dalrymple jerked it. Miss Tudno Watkins's head jerked painfully up and down.

'Agh! You fool, you're breaking my neck!' she protested.

More people came running up. Omelette emerged staggering from the cage plump with seed. He belched.

Lord Dalrymple bent down to help Miss Tudno Watkins to her feet. Omelette wasn't sure where he was. The sudden spinning of the cage following so swiftly upon a large meal made him feel sick. He collapsed in a heap between his Lordship and Miss Tudno Watkins who was still struggling to wrench the placard off her head.

'Eric!' cried Omelette. 'Help!'

Eric stuck his head from beneath what was left of the tablecloth. He saw his dear friend apparently being crushed to death between a thin man in a grey suit and a fat lady with a placard round her neck. The thin man's bottom was pointing most invitingly in his direction. For any self respecting goat an invitation such as this is not to be turned down. He sized up the tightly stretched striped

152

pants, lowered his head, took aim and charged. His aim was true. Lord Dalrymple and Miss Tudno Watkins shot across the marquee demolishing a table of prize-winning trifles and sponge cakes *en route*. The tablecloth fell over Eric's head. All was confusion. Outside the sound of a police siren could be heard.

The young girl leapt to her feet. 'Come on,' she cried. She picked up the still dazed Omelette and tucked him under her arm.

'Help, Eric,' cried Omelette. He struggled to free himself but the young girl had too strong a grip on him. He looked round. There was no sign of Eric. A large, white, tablecloth bucked and leapt amongst the spectators.

The young girl ducked under the flap of the tent and raced across the showground. A police car screamed to a halt, its blue light flashing. A policeman clambered out. He took out his note book.

'Where's the trouble?' he asked. Behind them the tent swayed and creaked. From within came muffled cries and squeaks. The poles swayed. The crowd held its breath. With a kind of sigh the tent slowly subsided and sat down sedately on the ground.

'Over there,' said a young girl, pointing at the collapsed tent.

The police raced away. Of Eric there was nothing to be seen.

The young girl flung herself into a truck and started the engine. She put the truck into gear and lurched forward, the engine roaring. The car spun and skidded in a large circle throwing up clods of earth. Omelette looked out of the window. Where was Eric? He caught a glimpse of a tablecloth blundering blindly across the field, before running into an icecream van – overturning it. The

153

tablecloth slipped to the ground. Underneath it was a goat.

'Eric,' screamed Omelette. 'Over here!'

The pick-up truck pulled away. Eric galloped after it. At the exit from the showground the pick-up stopped once more. Eric took off in a graceful leap. He landed with a crash at the back of the truck and slid, his front hooves stuck straight out in front of him. The back of the truck's cabin stopped his progress rather suddenly. Tyres burning, the girl screeched away.

They tore along main roads, down winding country lanes, through villages and under bridges. Omelette was hurled from side to side. Eventually they turned into a long drive with hedges on either side. Omelette had the feeling he had been here before. But he couldn't remember exactly. Then the girl drove into a farmyard past a hayrick. Omelette's heart beat faster. He knew that hayrick. He looked out of the other window. And that barn. The door was broken. Broken just as though a goat had attacked it. Could it be? Yes, he was sure. Home!

The young girl stopped the truck and tucking Omelette under her arm she strode up to the door and knocked. A grey-haired lady in a flowered pinafore came out of the door.

'Jenny!' she said in some surprise. 'I wasn't expecting you.'

'Hello, Mam, I wasn't expecting to come,' said Jenny.

Mrs Westmoreland peered at Omelette. 'What's that you got under your arm, gal?'

'It's for you.'

'For me?'

'It's a bantam. That dreadful Mrs Tudno Watkins was abusing it. I just snatched it up and ran. They're sure to come and look for him at my house. Could you hide him here for a bit?

'Hide him?' She looked closer at Omelette. 'Just a minute,' she said to Omelette, 'don't I know you?'

'You know him?' said Jenny in astonishment.

'You know him too, gal. Remember how he sat in your beret when he was a chick? Yes, me and him's old pals, ain't we, Omelette?' she said, stroking Omelette under the chin.

She called over her shoulder, 'Westy! Come here a minute.'

Mr Westmoreland emerged from the barn.

'Just look what our Jen brought in!' said Mrs Westmoreland. 'It's our Omelette.'

Mr Westmoreland joined them. When he saw Omelette he pushed back his cap and scratched his head.

'Well, would you credit it. It's that there Omelette. Well, I'll be blowed!'

Mrs Westmoreland turned Omelette round and looked him in the eye. 'Where you bin these two months, eh?'

'D'you mean he was one of the animals that was stolen by the brothers that night?' said Jenny. 'Those two that are in jail now in Haversham?'

'The very one,' said Mrs Westmoreland. 'I'd know him anywhere.'

'There's only one Omelette,' said Mr Westmoreland.

Mrs Westmoreland looked round. 'Those animals we lost, near all of 'em come back, you know. They found the van crashed four miles away the same night. Poor creatures wandering about the lane, lost and forlorn. They was bruised some of 'em. But they survived. Enoch there and Doris. 'Course one or two we lost. Omelette was one of 'em and now he's back.'

'And of course Eric,' said Mr Westmoreland sadly. 'We won't see him again, I reckon.'

At that moment Eric took it into his head to descend from the van and to walk in a princely fashion across the farmyard towards his house.

Mr Westmoreland removed his cap completely. 'Blow me sideways with an iron feather!' he exclaimed. 'If that doesn't beat all. Am I seeing things or summat? Is that a ghost or a goat?'

'That's no ghost, that's our Eric.'

And Eric walked past them as though it were the most normal thing in the world to go missing for two months and then to arrive home in the back of a truck. Omelette hopped down and trotted after him. He leapt on to his back.

Mrs Westmoreland shook her head. 'If only they could talk,' she said, 'what a story they could tell.' And they all went inside for a cup of tea and a lardy cake.

And Eric and Omelette sat by the stone wall overlooking the river as the red sun went down. Like old friends who have shared much and know one another well, they had no need to speak. They just sat and stared happily at the shifting clouds and the ever rolling river.

And then Omelette leapt up on to a stone wall and sang a song. It rang across the valley and up the farther hill.

'What was that about?' asked Eric.

Omelette looked at him. 'Home,' he said. 'Just home.'

'Ah yes, home,' said Eric. And they both smiled.

The echo died. And it seemed to them that from far away came an answering call. It reached into the sky and spread across the countryside. At the end came a special tra-lah-lah. The two friends looked at one another. They knew who it was and what it said. But they weren't telling.

Not yet anyway.